The Crystal Fox Saga

Book One: Whispers of a Shattered Balance

Christopher Plummer

CRYSTAL
FOX
PRESS

Crystal Fox Press

For all those who dream of balance, even when the world feels broken.
For the storytellers, the readers, and the ones who carry light through
shadow.
And for those who believed in the Crystal Fox from the very beginning
— this tale is yours as much as it is mine.
— Christopher Plummer

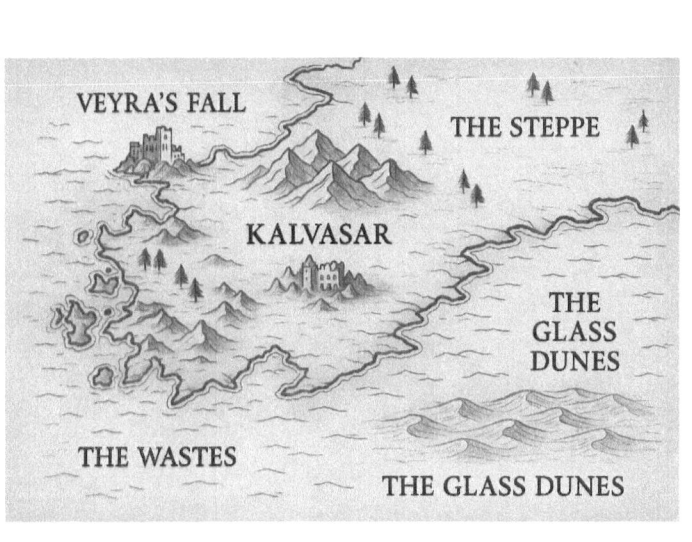

Contents

Chapter One

The Breaking of Balance

When the harmony of countless worlds is shattered, even a guardian's light can be chained in crystal

T he universes sang once.

It was not a song made of words, but of harmony—of countless worlds turning in quiet rhythm, tethered together by the radiant breath of the Eclipsera Stone. Where it shone, there was balance. Where it pulsed, there was peace. And where it was guarded, none dared bring ruin.

At the heart of this eternal vigil stood Princess Serenya, the warrior of dawn and dusk, clad in armor kissed by starlight. Her blade was not

forged of steel but of pure cosmic fire, and her oath was simple: protect
the Stone, and through it, protect all worlds.

But harmony, as all songs, carries dissonance.

From the edges of forgotten voids, where broken realities bled into
nothingness, he came. Avarith. Once a knight of light, now clad in
armor that gleamed black as a dragon's scale and bled fire like an open
wound. With him came the Draconis Order—seven warriors, each
armored in hues of terrible beauty, each bound to a power stolen from
creation itself.

The sky of Serenya's world burned the day they came.

She stood before the Stone, its glow bathing her in cerulean flame,
when the air itself cracked open. From the fissure stepped the Red
Dragon, helm shaped like a snarling beast, his gauntlets dripping
molten fire. Behind him, the Silver Dragon bent the light around her,
time stuttering with every step he took. The others followed, and last
came Avarith, his shadow devouring the glow of the Stone until the
chamber drowned in darkness.

"Balance," he said, his voice like iron drawn across stone, "is weakness. Order is strength. And strength belongs to those who seize it."

Serenya's blade leapt to life, its fire carving light into the gloom.
"You will not have it, Avarith. I swore an oath to all the worlds, and
through death I will keep it."

Their clash shattered the stars.

Steel against flame. Light against shadow. The warrior princess fought as though the multiverse itself guided her hand. Every strike of her blade split darkness, every breath summoned echoes of galaxies long past. She struck down the Green Dragon with a single arc of fire, drove back the Gold with her shield, and locked blades with the Red until the walls themselves wept flame.

But Avarith did not fight alone.

The Black Dragon's whispers clawed at her mind, dragging forth memories of her failures. The Silver Dragon bent her movements until her strikes faltered. The Azure Dragon wove illusions so real she saw her fallen comrades rise only to betray her again. Piece by piece, her strength was torn away—not by power, but by doubt.

When her knees struck the crystal floor, Avarith raised his hand. Shadows wound around her, burning as they bound.

"You guard peace," he said. "But peace is a chain. I will forge freedom in fire."

And before her eyes, the Eclipsera Stone broke.

Its light flared, then splintered into seven shards, each seized by the dragons. The harmony of the universes screamed as threads of reality tore apart. Stars guttered, worlds cracked, and time itself faltered in its step.

Serenya, last guardian of balance, cried out—and in that moment, the spell fell. Her body collapsed inward, her form twisting, shrinking, reshaping until a small blue fox lay trembling where a warrior once stood. With a gesture, Avarith raised a prison of crystal around her, suspending her in timeless stillness.

"You will watch," he promised. "You will see as your universes crumble, one by one, until none remember your name."

And with that, darkness claimed the throne of creation.

The song of balance was silenced.

The fox slept, and the worlds began to die.

Chapter Two

Whispers Through the Crystal

In silence unbroken, the fox dreams—her voice slipping into mortal hearts like threads of forgotten light

S ilence.

That was her prison.

Not the silence of peace, where birdsong might follow and rivers might flow. This was the silence of a wound—deep, aching, eternal. Within the crystal, time had no meaning. The warrior princess, now fox, felt the endless stillness press against her fur like a weight too heavy to breathe beneath. She could not move. She could not fight. She could only watch.

Through the fractures of her prison, she glimpsed the unraveling. Universes once bright with creation faded into shadow. Oceans turned to dust, stars drowned in their own light, and cities cracked into hollow echoes of stone. Each shard of the Eclipsera Stone, stolen by the Draconis Order, radiated a different corruption. The Red Dragon's fire scorched entire planets into lifeless cinders. The Black Dragon's whispers spread fear like plague, turning brother against brother until civilizations destroyed themselves. The Gold Dragon bent gravity so violently that moons tore themselves apart, raining ruin upon the worlds they once circled.

She could only watch.

But her spirit was not broken.

Bound in fox form, her essence still carried the ancient light she had sworn to guard. Though her voice could no longer pierce the waking world, it seeped into the realm of dreams—rivers of thought where even Avarith's shadows could not fully follow.

And so she whispered.

At first, her words were scattered, no more than fragments carried on the tides of slumber. Do not fear... the balance... still breathes... Dreams flickered with fleeting images: a blade of starlight, a fox of blue flame, a stone that sang. Most who dreamed dismissed it as nothing more than their own wandering mind. But in one soul, the whispers took root.

Far away, in a dying world where the skies bled crimson and the seas boiled to vapor, a boy stirred. His name was Kaelen—a farmer's son, no knight nor scholar, only a youth who had watched his village collapse into ash under the weight of the Draconis fire. He had nothing left but a handful of memories and the hollow ache of survival.

That night, the dream came.

He stood in a forest that should not exist, for his land had long since burned. The trees glowed with a silver luminescence, their leaves rustling though no wind blew. At the center of the clearing stood a crystal, tall as a mountain, glowing faintly with cerulean light. And within, he saw it: a fox with fur of sapphire fire, eyes burning with sorrow—and with hope.

The fox lifted its gaze, and though no sound broke the dream's silence, Kaelen heard.

"Child of the ashes... hear me."

The words struck like thunder within his chest. He fell to his knees, unable to look away.

"The balance has fallen. The universes fracture. But you... you still remain. You are not chosen by blood, nor by prophecy, but by endurance. You have lived where others have fallen. Will you bear the light I cannot carry?"

Kaelen's lips trembled. "I... I am no warrior."

The fox's eyes softened, the glow of her prison pulsing faintly.

"Neither was I... until I became one."

The dream shuddered. Darkness rippled at the edges, shadows coiling like serpents—Avarith's corruption, slithering even into sleep. The fox's form flickered, as if straining to hold the dream together.

"Seek me," she urged, her voice now desperate. "Follow the flame. Across the ruins, across the stars—you will find me. Break the crystal, and the worlds may yet be healed."

The darkness surged, swallowing the silver forest. Kaelen's body felt as though it were being dragged beneath the waves. The last thing he saw was the fox's eyes—burning, pleading, eternal.

And then he woke.

The world around him was still broken. Ash still choked the sky. But in his palm, clenched so tightly his skin bled, there burned a fragment of blue fire that had followed him from the dream.

The whisper echoed once more, softer now, but clear:

"Find me..."

Chapter Three

The Ash-Bound Wanderer

Flames of a Broken World

K aelen awoke to the sting of smoke in his throat and the sight of the world he had always known—broken.

The crimson sky never faded, painted by the Red Dragon's conquest. Forests had been reduced to blackened husks. Rivers hissed steam where they once flowed, poisoned by molten rock. Villages like his had been erased, scattered into ruins where only scavengers dared tread.

Yet when he looked down at his hand, he saw it: the faint flicker of blue flame, cool and steady, cradled in his palm like a heartbeat. It was no illusion. No fever dream. The whisper of the fox had crossed the barrier of sleep and into waking.

He clenched it tightly.

"Find me," the voice echoed again, soft but insistent.

For the first time since the fire claimed his home, Kaelen felt something stir in his chest other than grief.

Hope.

He began to walk.

At first, there was no direction, only instinct. The flame pulsed faintly whenever he strayed too far from the path, dimming if he hesitated, glowing brighter when his feet found the right road. He followed it past scorched farmlands and broken towers, through the bones of cities that had once been alive with music. The further he walked, the more he realized how deep the corruption ran.

The air itself carried the Red Dragon's taint—dry, heavy, burning. Kaelen passed fields where shadows moved against the wind, echoes of people who had perished screaming, left behind as living nightmares. Even in daylight, he could hear them whispering. It's hopeless. You cannot fight them. You will fall as we did.

Yet the blue flame pushed them back, a lantern in a world of dread.

On the third night, he dreamed again.

The fox was there, dimmer than before, but her eyes still sharp. The crystal walls pulsed faintly around her, as if his steps brought her strength.

"You walk the path," she whispered. "And yet it is only the beginning. Others must walk with you."

Kaelen frowned. "Others? There's no one left. Not here. The Draconis have taken everything."

"Not all. Some endure. Some resist. As you do." The fox's tail lashed once against the crystal. "Seek the river that bleeds silver. There, one waits who has not yet broken."

The dream fractured, fading into shadow before Kaelen could ask more.

He found it the next evening.

Through the cracked stone of the world, water still trickled—a stream that shimmered unnaturally in the dim light, glowing faint silver as though reflecting a moon that no longer rose. And kneeling at its edge was a figure.

She was older than him by a handful of years, her cloak torn and blackened, her hair tangled with soot. A staff lay across her knees, carved with runes that glowed faintly with the same hue as the water.

She was whispering words Kaelen did not understand, her eyes closed in concentration.

When she finally opened them, they glowed faintly green.

Kaelen froze.

"You're... not one of them," she said, her voice hoarse but firm. "You're no dragon."

"I..." Kaelen raised his hands, unsure what to say. "I'm just—"

"You carry light," she interrupted, her eyes narrowing at the blue flame pulsing in his palm. She studied it as though recognizing a secret she had long forgotten. "Not a torch. Not fire. Something older."

Kaelen hesitated, then asked, "Who are you?"

The woman gripped her staff tightly, as if the name cost her something to say.

"Lysera. Once a healer. Now... nothing."

Kaelen shook his head. "Not nothing. She told me I'd find someone here."

Lysera's gaze sharpened. "She? Who?"

Kaelen lifted his hand, the blue flame dancing like a living thing.

"The fox."

For the first time, Lysera's face changed—not to suspicion, but to awe.

"You've seen her," she whispered. "The guardian in the crystal. I thought... I thought she was only a story."

"She's real," Kaelen said, feeling the weight of his own conviction for the first time. "And she's calling for us."

That night, by the silver stream, Kaelen told Lysera of his dreams. Of the blue fox, the crystal, the whispers of balance. Lysera listened without speaking, her fingers tracing the runes on her staff, as though weighing his words against the lore she once knew.

When he finished, she finally spoke.

"Then perhaps the universes are not yet lost. If the guardian still speaks, she still fights. And if she fights... then so must we."

The flame in Kaelen's palm flared brighter, as though answering her words.

Far away, deep within her crystal, Serenya stirred. For the first time since her imprisonment, the silence cracked with the faintest sound—her heartbeat.

Chapter Four

Ashes of the Red Dragon

Through Ash, the Flame Endures

The silver stream wound westward, leading them across a land scorched to ruin. For three days, Kaelen and Lysera walked in silence, broken only by the sound of their weary steps and the crackle of fires still smoldering across the horizon. The blue flame in Kaelen's palm grew stronger, its glow steady and urgent, as if it were guiding them toward something.

On the fourth night, the air changed.

Smoke thickened, bitter and metallic. The ground blackened into cracked obsidian. Overhead, the sky no longer bled crimson—it burned, churning with waves of fire that twisted into the shape of wings.

Lysera gripped her staff. "We are entering the Red Dragon's reach."

Kaelen felt his chest tighten. The stories of the Red Dragon—Draconis general of fire and destruction—were whispered even in his ruined village. He was said to leave behind not just death, but a hunger in the land itself, so that nothing would ever grow again.

The fox's whisper came faint in his mind, like a breeze through the smoke:

Do not turn away. His shard poisons this world. To heal it, you must face him.

They climbed a ridge of black stone and saw what had once been a city. Now it was a charred carcass, towers melted into twisted spires, streets glowing with rivers of magma. At its heart stood a massive forge, its chimneys spewing flame into the heavens.

And at the forge's peak stood the Red Dragon.

His armor was blood-red, scales interlocked like the hide of some ancient beast. Flames seeped from the cracks between his plates, and his helm was crowned with horns like molten spears. In one hand he carried a war-axe taller than Kaelen himself, its edge glowing white-hot.

The sight of him made Kaelen stumble. Every instinct screamed to run.

But Lysera's hand steadied him. Her voice was low, but unyielding. "Fear is his weapon. If you bow to it, he has already won."

Kaelen swallowed hard, then nodded.

The Red Dragon turned. His voice was a furnace, rumbling through the ruins.

"Another world's carrion wanders into my ash. Did you come to burn, little ones?"

Lysera raised her staff, green light flaring against the red glow. "We came to end your plague."

The dragon knight laughed, a sound like molten rock splitting. He leapt from the forge, landing with a shockwave that cracked the earth around them.

Kaelen nearly fell, but the blue flame surged, steadying his body. He felt it flow into his veins, carrying not strength, but clarity. The whisper of the fox echoed once more:

Do not fight fire with fire. Fight it with what endures.

The battle began.

Lysera moved first, striking her staff into the ground. Vines burst from cracks in the obsidian, glowing with faint emerald light, wrapping around the Red Dragon's legs. He roared, flames blasting outward, burning the vines to ash—but they slowed him for a heartbeat.

Kaelen seized the moment. Guided by the blue flame, he hurled a shard of light from his palm. It struck the knight's armor and shattered harmlessly, but the flare made the giant recoil for an instant.

It wasn't much. But it was enough to prove one thing: the fox's power could touch even a Draconis general.

The Red Dragon snarled, flames rolling from his armor. "You carry her light." His voice dropped into a growl. "Then you will die screaming."

He raised his axe, and the ground split in a wave of fire that raced toward them. Kaelen dove aside, the heat searing his skin, but Lysera stood firm. She drove her staff into the wave, splitting the flames around her in two streams.

Her strength was waning—Kaelen could see it in her trembling hands. But he could also see the fox's blue flame pulsing in his own.

He realized, with sudden clarity, that the flame was not a weapon. It was a bond. His survival, his endurance, his courage—that was its power. And if he could share it...

"Lysera!" he shouted, thrusting his hand toward her. The blue flame leapt from his palm into her staff.

The runes carved into the wood blazed to life, glowing with blue fire woven into green. The staff pulsed, alive with a force Lysera had never felt before.

Together, they struck.

The staff slammed into the ground, vines erupting once more—but this time they burned with blue light. They coiled around the Red Dragon's limbs, and this time, his fire could not consume them. The flame of endurance held fast.

The knight roared, thrashing against the bonds. "This will not hold me!"

Kaelen raised his voice, trembling but unbroken. "It doesn't have to. It only has to last."

And for the first time since his imprisonment, Serenya—watching from the crystal across the universes—smiled.

Chapter Five

The Scars of Fire

Where Flames Leave Their Mark

The vines of blue and green light strained against the Red Dragon's burning armor. For a moment, it seemed as though the impossible had been achieved—the general slowed, held, his flames sputtering under the weight of their combined power.

But only for a moment.

With a roar that shook the ruined city, the Red Dragon flexed, and the air itself combusted. The vines exploded in a storm of ash. Lysera was thrown back, tumbling across the obsidian ground, her staff clattering from her hands. Kaelen was blasted to his knees, the blue flame in his palm flickering dangerously.

The Red Dragon advanced, each step leaving molten footprints. "You have strength, little embers," he growled, raising his axe high. "But strength is not enough."

Kaelen's breath caught. His body screamed to run, but his legs would not move. He looked to Lysera—struggling to rise, smoke curling from her cloak—and felt the crushing truth: they were not ready.

The fox's whisper surged into his mind, sharp and urgent.

Not victory. Survival. Take her and flee.

The axe fell—

—but Lysera thrust out her hand, and the ground beneath them cracked open. A surge of roots, glowing faintly blue with Kaelen's lingering flame, burst upward, striking the Red Dragon's chest. The impact staggered him for only a breath, but it was enough.

"Run!" Lysera shouted, grabbing Kaelen's arm.

They fled into the ruined streets, the earth trembling with every step the Red Dragon gave chase. Fire rained from the forge behind them, rivers of molten stone pouring down the roads. Buildings collapsed around them, shadows writhing in the inferno.

Kaelen's lungs burned, his legs barely carrying him. But the flame pulsed again, urging him forward. Through alleys of rubble, across bridges half-melted by fire, until at last the ruined city fell behind them and the night swallowed them whole.

Only when the Red Dragon's roar faded into the distance did they collapse on the blackened plain.

Kaelen lay on his back, staring at the blood-red sky. His chest heaved with every breath, and his hands shook violently.

Lysera sat nearby, her face pale, soot smeared across her skin. She held her staff close, though the runes had dimmed again. Her voice was quiet, but steady.

"We cannot fight him. Not yet."

Kaelen swallowed hard, the memory of the Red Dragon's burning eyes still seared into his mind. He wanted to deny it, to shout that they had to fight, that they couldn't let the worlds burn. But the truth was plain: if Lysera hadn't pulled him away, they would both already be ash.

The fox's whisper came again, softer now, but filled with resolve.

You have taken the first step. The generals are not invincible, but their power is greater than yours. You must find others. Gather those who endure. Only together can you reclaim the Stone.

Kaelen closed his eyes. He could still feel the heat of the dragon's fire, the hopeless weight of facing such power. But beneath that fear burned the flame—the same light that had carried him this far.

He sat up, his voice low but firm. "Then we'll find them. Whoever's left. However long it takes."

Lysera met his gaze, and for the first time since they met, a faint smile curved her lips.

In the crystal, Serenya's tail curled softly around her body. She could not break free—not yet—but the bond between her whispers and Kaelen's heart had grown stronger. Through him, through Lysera, the balance still had a chance to be restored.

And so the fox waited. And watched.

The Red Dragon roared again in the distance, a promise of battles yet to come.

But Kaelen and Lysera lived.
And that, for now, was victory enough.

Chapter Six

The Shadow of a Thief

Where Trust Walks in Shadows

The world beyond the Red Dragon's forge was quieter, though no less broken. For days, Kaelen and Lysera walked across scarred plains where grass would never grow again, drinking from poisoned streams and resting beneath skies cracked with fire. Each night, Kaelen dreamed of the fox in the crystal. Each morning, the flame in his palm urged him onward.

Others remain, she whispered. Those who endure not through strength, but through cunning... through knowledge... through defiance. Seek them.

Lysera interpreted the message as they traveled. "The guardian means we cannot survive on courage alone. We need minds and skills the dragons cannot predict. And there is one place left where such a soul might hide."

They turned their steps toward a broken city that once thrived as a hub of trade: Veyra's Reach.

What remained of Veyra's Reach was a labyrinth of shattered towers, alleys filled with smoke, and bridges collapsing into rivers of black water. Yet amid the ruins, life still scuttled—figures cloaked in rags, gangs that prowled the shadows, and whispered rumors of a thief who defied even the Draconis patrols.

Kaelen and Lysera heard the tale at a crumbling inn, where weary survivors bartered scraps of food for silence.

"They say he wears the shadows like a second skin," muttered an old merchant. "The Red Dragon's men hunt him, but never catch him. Slips through their claws like smoke. Some call him traitor. Others call him savior. I say he's a curse that'll get us all killed."

The merchant's words were punctuated by a distant crash—guards in crimson armor smashing through the streets, their torches lighting the night.

Kaelen looked to Lysera. She gave a faint nod. "If he can evade them, he may be the ally the fox spoke of."

They found him at midnight.

A Draconis patrol had cornered a group of survivors in a collapsed marketplace, their dragon-helmed leader preparing to execute them as an example. Before Kaelen or Lysera could act, a blur moved across the rooftops. A shadow leapt, landed, and with a flick of steel, the leader's torch was snuffed out.

Chaos erupted. Knives glinted in the dark. Chains snapped loose. When the smoke cleared, the guards were unconscious, bound in their own armor, and the survivors had fled.

The shadow stood in their place.

He was lean, cloaked in black, his face half-covered by a scarf. His eyes gleamed amber in the firelight, sharp and calculating. He twirled a dagger once before sheathing it, his voice smooth but edged.

"You've been following me."

Kaelen froze. "How—?"

The thief smirked. "Your footsteps are loud. Your light even louder." He gestured toward Kaelen's hand, where the faint blue flame still pulsed. "That's going to get you killed here."

Lysera stepped forward, unafraid. "We didn't come to hunt you. We came to find you."

The thief raised a brow. "Flattered, but I don't do charity. Whatever fight you're chasing, I'm not interested."

"You already fight," Kaelen said, surprising himself. "You saved those people. You defied the Draconis. That means you are interested."

The thief's eyes narrowed. For a moment, Kaelen thought he would vanish into the shadows. But instead, the man gave a dry laugh.

"You've got fire, kid. Dangerous fire. Fine. You want me in your fight? Then prove you can survive it."

Before Kaelen could ask what he meant, a horn blared in the distance. Flames rose as more Draconis patrols marched toward the marketplace. The thief drew two blades, their edges glinting like fangs.

"Welcome to Veyra's Reach," he said. "Let's see if your light burns, or if it just gets us both killed."

Chapter Seven

Blades in the Smoke

Where Shadows Clash, Truth Cuts Deep

The horns grew louder, echoing through the broken streets of Veyra's Reach. Torches flared in the distance, shadows of armored Draconis soldiers stretching across the ruins.

The thief spun his daggers once and grinned beneath his scarf. "Rule number one," he said, voice low and quick, "keep moving. Stop for even a breath, and you'll burn."

Then he bolted into the night.

Kaelen and Lysera had no choice but to follow.

The thief moved like smoke—slipping through alleys, vaulting over collapsed walls, darting across half-fallen bridges with barely a sound. His cloak blended into the darkness, his steps so light they seemed unreal.

Kaelen, in contrast, stumbled. His boots cracked stone, his breath came ragged, and the blue flame in his palm pulsed frantically, guiding him where his eyes couldn't see. Lysera fared better, her staff striking the ground in rhythm with her steps, green runes flaring to push aside rubble or collapse pathways behind them.

"Faster!" the thief hissed, as arrows clattered against the walls near them. "They've marked your light!"

Kaelen glanced down at the flame in his palm—still burning bright. "I can't hide it!"

"Then you'd better outrun it!"

They ducked into a narrow street lined with leaning towers, their windows glowing faint with embers. The thief led them up a broken stairwell, three flights at a sprint, then leapt through a shattered window into open air. Kaelen's heart lurched as the thief landed gracefully on a rope stretched between two rooftops and ran across it as though it were solid ground.

"You've got to be joking," Kaelen muttered.

Lysera gave him a look—half warning, half challenge—then stepped onto the rope, her staff balancing her as she crossed.

Kaelen hesitated only a moment before following, the flame in his hand flickering wildly. The rope swayed, the drop yawning below like a hungry mouth. His arms flailed, his heart thundered, but some-how—somehow—he made it across.

The thief was waiting on the far roof, smirking. "Not terrible."

Before Kaelen could catch his breath, the roof beneath them shook—Draconis soldiers had scaled the towers, their crimson armor glowing in the firelight.

The thief sighed, spinning his blades. "Rule number two: when cornered... strike first."

He moved like lightning. One moment he was still, the next he was a blur, blades flashing in arcs of silver. He struck with precision, never wasting movement. Soldiers fell back, stunned, their armor cut in weak joints Kaelen wouldn't have thought vulnerable.

Lysera joined the fray, vines lashing from her staff to drag enemies off balance. Kaelen, heart pounding, raised his hand and hurled a burst of blue light. It struck a soldier square in the chest, knocking him back over the edge of the roof.

But for every soldier that fell, more climbed the walls.

"We can't hold here!" Lysera shouted.

The thief nodded. "Exactly. Rule number three: escape is an art."

He slashed through a rope tethering part of the tower's wreckage. The structure groaned, then collapsed into the street below with a thunderous crash—bridging a gap between rooftops. Smoke and dust exploded outward, cloaking the night.

"Move!" he barked.

They sprinted across the fallen wreckage, smoke curling around them. The soldiers, blinded and coughing, fired arrows wildly into the haze, but the trio was already gone—vanishing into the maze of ruins.

At last, after what felt like hours, they dropped into a hidden alcove beneath a half-collapsed bridge. The thief crouched, pulling back his scarf to reveal a face hardened by years of survival but marked with a sharp, almost playful grin.

"You two aren't completely hopeless," he said. "Slow, loud, reckless... but not hopeless." He extended a hand. "Name's Darek. And since you kept up—barely—I'll hear your offer."

Kaelen, still breathless, glanced at Lysera. She gave the faintest nod. He took Darek's hand, the flame in his palm flaring briefly as if sealing the pact.

From deep within her crystal prison, Serenya stirred once more. Through Kaelen, through Lysera, through this thief who had chosen shadows instead of surrender, her reach was growing.

And in the distance, unseen by any of them, another pair of dragon-helmed eyes watched the ruins with cold amusement.

The hunt had only just begun.

Chapter Eight

Council of Dragons

Whispers of Betrayal

F ar from the broken alleys of Veyra's Reach, beyond the sight of mortal eyes, stood the Obsidian Spire—a fortress forged in the void between worlds. Its walls breathed shadow. Its towers clawed at the stars. And within its highest hall, firelight burned upon scaled armor.

The Draconis Order had gathered.

Seven thrones encircled a dais of black crystal. Upon the dais, mounted like a trophy, floated one of the fractured shards of the Eclipsera Stone, pulsing with sickly red light.

The Red Dragon knelt before it, his armor still scorched where Kaelen and Lysera's vines had held him. His voice rumbled through the chamber.

"They were nothing. A boy. A woman with a staff. And yet..." His gauntlet clenched into a fist. "...they carried her light."

A ripple of whispers passed among the others.

The Azure Dragon, clad in shimmering blue scales that shifted like liquid, leaned forward. "Impossible. The guardian is sealed. Her light should be bound in crystal." His voice was smooth, but his eyes were sharp with unease.

"Bound, yes," purred the Black Dragon, his armor swallowing the firelight. Shadows twisted at his feet like living smoke. "But whispers linger. Dreams are treacherous. Perhaps she calls out even from her prison."

The Silver Dragon scoffed, his helm gleaming like polished moonlight. "Let her whisper. A fox in a cage is no threat. What can a dream do against the Order?"

The Red Dragon's reply was a growl. "A dream drove me to the edge of defeat."

That silenced the chamber.

At the head of the circle, upon the tallest throne, sat Avarith. His obsidian armor glowed faintly with veins of molten fire, his dragon-helm crowned with spines that curved like a crown. He had listened in silence, but now his voice filled the hall like thunder.

"Do not mistake sparks for fire." His gaze swept over them, burning through their armor as though seeing into their cores. "But do not dismiss them, either. The guardian's light cannot be ignored. If it has found hosts, then it has chosen vessels to carry its flame."

The Gold Dragon leaned forward, his voice heavy as gravity itself. "Then they must be crushed now. Before they spread."

Avarith's helm tilted, as though amused. "Crushed, yes. But not too quickly." His hand rose, and the shard of the Stone flared, casting twisted light across the chamber. "Fear is a more enduring weapon than death. Let the mortals see their champions rise... only to fall. Let them watch hope burn again."

The generals bowed their heads.

But the Black Dragon's shadows stirred restlessly, whispering through the chamber: They grow bolder. The fox's song is not yet silenced. We must be swift.

Avarith's voice cut like a blade. "Patience. The guardian's chosen will crawl toward their doom, and when they do, we will be waiting. Each general will claim their turn, until even her whispers are ash."

The shard's glow dimmed, and the hall fell silent.

But in the void between worlds, where the Stone's fragments pulsed their corruption, the balance quivered—thin, fragile, straining against collapse.

The sparks had been noticed.

The hunt had truly begun.

Chapter Nine

Cries Beneath the Crystal

Whispers of Power, Shadows of War

D arkness pressed in on every side.

For Serenya, time had no meaning anymore. Within the crystal prison, the flow of moments was like sand caught in still water—shifting, yet frozen. Her body was gone, replaced by the spectral shape of a fox curled in shimmering blue light. Her soul, though, still burned as the Warrior Princess of the Multiverse, guardian of balance.

And she felt them.

The meeting in the Obsidian Spire pulsed through the fragments of the stolen Eclipsera Stone, each shard echoing its master's intent. Their voices—distorted, heavy with dragonfire and shadow—slithered into her prison.

The Red Dragon's fury.
The Azure's suspicion.
The Black's cold hunger.
The Silver's arrogance.
The Gold's merciless certainty.
And above all, the Dark Lord Avarith—commanding, unshakable, his will like chains tightening around every universe.

Their words became firebrands pressed against her spirit:

"A fox in a cage is no threat."
"Crush the vessels before they spread."
"Let hope rise... so it may burn."

Serenya pressed against the crystal walls, claws of light scraping at its surface. It held fast. Always it held. She had fought gods and tyrants, had carried her blade into wars that spanned galaxies, but now she could not even break glass.

Her voice echoed only inward, swallowed by the prison. Yet, faintly—like ripples cast on still water—her cries escaped into the dreams of mortals.

Kaelen had heard her. Lysera too. And now... perhaps even the thief.

But the generals' laughter shook her core. Their certainty was poison, and the worst of it was that she felt the truth of their confidence. Kaelen was not ready. Lysera's power was still raw. They had escaped, but only just. Against a general at full strength... they would fall.

Her spirit flickered, dimming for a moment as despair clawed its way in. The multiverse itself shuddered in her silence. Whole worlds, once held in harmony by her vigilance, had begun to crumble—oceans boiling, skies blackening, suns collapsing in on themselves. She could sense them all, but could save none.

"Please..." her whisper bled into the void. "Don't let them bear this weight alone."

The crystal pulsed in answer, not with freedom, but with the faintest shimmer—like a star seen through stormclouds. It was not escape. It was not power. But it was connection.

Through that shimmer, she felt Kaelen's exhaustion, Lysera's determination, and Darek's wary grin. They were alive. They had not turned away.

Her heart, even in its spectral form, steadied.

"They think I am silenced." Her fox-shape raised its head, eyes glowing brighter. "But even a whisper can become a storm."

The crystal trembled—not with breaking, but with defiance. Avarith's laughter echoed one last time, but this time she answered.

Her voice rippled through the dream-currents, reaching for Kaelen, Lysera, and whoever else destiny would bring.

"Find each other. Grow stronger. I will guide you. I will not be silent."

And though the walls of her prison remained unbroken, the faintest crack of light spread outward—so thin it would be invisible to any Draconis eye. But in the realm of dreams, it was a beacon.

The war for balance had not ended. It had only changed its shape.

Chapter Ten

Trial by Shadow

Only in Darkness, the True Light Shines

They rested in the hollow beneath the broken bridge until dawn bled across the ruins. Kaelen slept only in fragments, the blue flame pulsing faintly in his hand, while Lysera leaned on her staff in a half-doze. Darek, however, seemed tireless—eyes sharp, watching the streets above.

When the light finally came, pale and weak through the ash-stained sky, the thief rose.

"Last night proved you can keep up," he said. "But surviving one chase doesn't mean you're worth dying for. If you want me in your fight, you'll earn it."

Kaelen frowned. "How?"

Darek's grin was sharp as a blade. "By passing my test."

He led them deep into the maze of Veyra's Reach, where collapsed towers formed jagged alleys and shadows clung like cobwebs. At last, he stopped before what looked like the remnants of an old vault—its stone doors cracked but still standing.

"Inside," Darek said, pointing. "The Draconis use this ruin as a treasury. Food, water, relics... whatever they strip from survivors ends up here before being shipped to their generals. You want me on your side? Then prove you can take something back from them."

Lysera's brow furrowed. "You're asking us to steal from a Draconis stronghold."

"Exactly." Darek's amber eyes gleamed. "If you can't, you're not ready to fight generals. If you can, maybe you're worth my time."

Kaelen felt his stomach tighten. They had barely escaped the Red Dragon alive. But the fox's whisper stirred faintly inside him:

Every trial shapes you. Do not fear the test.

He nodded. "We'll do it."

The vault was guarded by three Draconis soldiers in scaled crimson armor. Their horns glowed faintly, weapons dripping with molten heat.

Darek crouched above on a ledge, whispering down. "First rule of shadows: don't fight what you don't have to. Slip past. Make them look the wrong way while you move the right one."

Kaelen and Lysera exchanged a look. Then, following Darek's signals, they crept forward.

Lysera tapped her staff gently against the ground, runes flaring just enough to stir dust further down the alley. The guards' heads snapped toward the sound, stepping away from the door. Kaelen's pulse hammered, but the flame in his palm glowed steady, guiding his feet soundlessly across the rubble.

They reached the vault door. Darek dropped down beside them, smirking. "Not bad. Now the hard part."

With a flick of his wrist, tools appeared in his hands. He worked the cracked lock swiftly, listening to the tumblers grind. "Cover me," he muttered.

Kaelen crouched low, flame ready, while Lysera wove a veil of vines and ash to blur their shapes. The seconds stretched. One guard began to turn back—Kaelen's breath caught—

Click. The vault groaned open.

Inside, crates of supplies lay stacked in shadow. But at the center, resting on a stone pedestal, was something stranger: a shard of crystal, faintly pulsing red. Kaelen felt its corruption instantly—it was a fragment of the Stone's power, twisted by Draconis hands.

His flame flared, almost leaping toward it.

Darek hissed. "Don't touch what you don't understand."

But Lysera shook her head. "This is part of why we're here. Every shard matters."

The moment stretched. Kaelen stepped forward, reaching toward the shard—

And the guards outside roared, having spotted them.

The vault erupted into chaos.

Chapter Eleven

Ashes and Shards

From Ruin, the Path Reforged

T he guards roared as they stormed into the vault, their crimson armor glowing with heat.

Kaelen didn't think—he moved. His hand seized the shard from the pedestal. The crystal burned cold against his palm, a poison pulse crawling up his arm, but the blue flame surged to meet it, wrapping the shard in light.

The guards froze at the sight, their voices distorted within their helms. "The fox's flame...!"

"Run!" Darek barked, already hurling a dagger into the nearest soldier's visor. The blade struck true, staggering the man as smoke hissed from the crack in his helm. Lysera slammed her staff to the ground, vines bursting from the stone to coil around the others' legs, slowing their charge.

Together, they bolted into the streets.

The city erupted around them—alarms blaring, horns echoing as Draconis patrols converged. Kaelen clutched the shard tight against his chest, the flame in his palm keeping its corruption at bay. Lysera's staff shone bright, vines lashing aside collapsing debris, while Darek guided them like a phantom through twisting alleys and shattered arches.

At one turn, Kaelen nearly stumbled into a patrol, but Darek pulled him back, muttering, "Rule four—shadows are louder than steel if you know how to use them." With a flick of his wrist, he dropped a smoke bomb that swallowed the street in choking fog, and they slipped away unseen.

They climbed broken rooftops, leapt narrow gaps, slid down fractured walls—every step a race against the red glow of pursuit. Soldiers shouted below, torches searching, but they were always one step behind.

Finally, with lungs burning and muscles screaming, the trio ducked into a collapsed aqueduct that opened into the wastelands beyond the city. The shouts faded behind them. The horns grew distant. Silence returned.

They had escaped.

In the shelter of the aqueduct, Kaelen sank against the stone, the shard still pulsing in his hands. Its light was sickly red, but the blue flame contained it, preventing its corruption from spreading.

Lysera knelt beside him, her hand brushing his arm. "You carried it without breaking. That proves the fox's light runs deeper in you than we knew."

Darek leaned against the wall, arms crossed, eyes glinting in the half-light. His smirk was back, but softer now.

"You're reckless," he said, "louder than a drunk giant, and you almost got us all killed."

Kaelen bristled, but before he could answer, Darek added, "But you did it. You took the shard. And that means maybe—just maybe—you're worth following."

He stepped forward and clapped Kaelen on the shoulder. "Name's Darek, and I'm in. Don't make me regret it."

Kaelen managed a tired grin. Lysera allowed herself the faintest smile.

And deep within her crystal, Serenya's fox-shape stirred, feeling the resonance of the reclaimed shard. For the first time since her fall, a piece of the Eclipsera Stone had slipped from the Order's grasp. It was not enough to restore balance—but it was a beginning.

The whispers of the fox reached Kaelen's dreams that night, warmer than ever before:

"You are not alone. The light grows."

Chapter Twelve

The Hunter Unleashed

The Hunt That Awakens the Flame

The Obsidian Spire trembled with fury.

On the dais of black crystal, the shard stolen from Veyra's Reach glowed faintly, its connection to the others broken. A ripple of weakness pulsed through the Draconis Order, small but undeniable.

The generals had gathered again, their scaled armor reflecting the blood-red light of the shards. The Red Dragon's roar still echoed in the chamber.

"They dared," he snarled. "Mortals tore a shard from our grasp. I will return and burn their ashes into the stone!"

But Avarith raised a single gauntleted hand, and silence fell.

"No. You already failed once. Your flames are too loud. This calls for another."

His gaze turned, slow and deliberate, to the shadows where the Black Dragon sat, cloaked in silence. His armor seemed carved from void, edges shifting as if they were smoke rather than steel. When he moved, it was like a ripple across water—unnatural, soundless.

The Black Dragon inclined his head. "You would have me hunt them."

"They carry the guardian's light," Avarith said, his voice iron and fire. "But light cannot burn where shadow reigns. Track them. Break their minds. Drag them back in chains if you wish—but make their deaths a story whispered in fear."

The Black Dragon rose. When he spoke, the chamber chilled.

"Hope is a fragile flame," he murmured. "I will snuff it before it spreads."

In her crystal prison, Serenya's fox-shape shivered. Through the fractures of the Eclipsera Stone, she felt the decision, the shifting of power. Shadows coiled across the threads of fate, reaching outward like talons.

Her whisper surged, desperate, carrying across the dream-currents:

Kaelen... Lysera... beware. He comes.

Far from the Spire, Kaelen startled awake in the darkness of the aqueduct. His flame burned suddenly brighter, trembling in his palm. Lysera stirred beside him, frowning, and Darek's eyes opened instantly, hand on his blade.

"What is it?" the thief asked.

Kaelen's voice was low, shaking. "We're being hunted."

In the silence that followed, a chill spread through the ruins outside—the kind of silence that comes not before fire, but before the cold weight of a nightmare.

The Black Dragon was on the move.

Chapter Thirteen

Shadows in Pursuit

When the Hunter Becomes the Hunted

The ruins were quiet. Too quiet.

Kaelen, Lysera, and Darek moved through the wastelands beyond Veyra's Reach, their stolen shard bound in cloth and carried close. The wind whistled through hollow stone, carrying the scent of smoke and ash. Yet beneath it, Kaelen felt something colder—like a presence pressing against his chest.

The fox's whisper stirred faintly in his mind. *He is near.*

That night, as they camped beneath the shell of a collapsed watch-tower, the shadows shifted. At first it seemed the firelight played tricks, stretching their shapes unnaturally long. But then one of the shadows broke free, slithering across the wall with a will of its own.

Lysera gasped, raising her staff. "Something's wrong—"

Darek cursed, drawing his blades. "We're being watched."

The fire sputtered, dimmed, and then *died*.

Darkness swallowed them whole.

Kaelen heard the voice first—low, smooth, filled with a venom that seeped into the bones.

"Little sparks," it whispered. "So bold, to steal from dragons. Did you think your defiance would go unseen?"

Kaelen's pulse raced. He turned, searching the black, but saw nothing. Only more shadows.

Then the illusions began.

From the dark, shapes emerged: figures from Kaelen's village, faces twisted in terror, crying out as fire consumed them. He saw his mother reaching for him, her hands burning to ash. He staggered back, heart breaking all over again.

"No," he whispered. "This isn't real—"

Lysera was caught in her own vision. Her staff trembled as she saw patients she once healed, rising from their graves with hollow eyes. Their voices accused her: *You couldn't save us. You never saved anyone.*

She cried out, striking at phantoms that dissolved into mist.

Darek stood rigid, his daggers ready, but even he faltered when a shadow stepped forward wearing his own face. "You'll betray them," it hissed. "Like you betrayed the last ones who trusted you."

The thief's hands shook.

Then the Black Dragon appeared.

His form coalesced from the shadows themselves, armor dark as night, helm crowned with horns like a predator's skull. His eyes glowed ember-red in the void, his voice echoing inside their skulls.

"You are nothing. Just prey. And prey cannot escape the hunter."

He raised a gauntlet, and the shadows lunged.

Kaelen's flame burst to life, piercing the illusions for an instant. The phantom villagers vanished. Lysera's dead returned to dust. The second Darek fell back, his double dissolved into smoke.

The Black Dragon recoiled slightly, narrowing his gaze at the glow in Kaelen's hand.

"The fox..." he hissed. "She dares."

The flame flickered, straining against the oppressive dark, but it held. Kaelen, shaking, lifted it high.

"We're not prey," he said, his voice trembling but unbroken. "Not anymore."

The Black Dragon's laughter was a cold wind that cut to the bone. "We shall see."

And as quickly as he had come, his form dissolved, vanishing back into the shadows. But the cold remained, a promise that the hunt was far from over.

The three companions sat in silence, their breaths heavy, the weight of the encounter pressing on them.

Lysera whispered, voice raw, "He'll never stop."

Darek's jaw tightened. "Then neither can we."

Kaelen closed his eyes, gripping the shard and the flame together. He could still hear Serenya's whisper faintly:

He hunts. But even hunters can bleed.

Chapter Fourteen

Fangs of the Shadow

In the Jaws of Shadow, Light Endures

T he night did not return to silence.

Even after the Black Dragon's form melted into mist, the ruins whispered with movement. The shadows *stayed wrong*—thicker, heavier, clinging to every wall. Kaelen's flame flickered weakly, fighting against an encroaching dark that seemed alive.

"He didn't leave," Darek muttered, blades at the ready. "He's waiting."

The fox's whisper trembled in Kaelen's mind. *Do not flee. If you run, the shadows follow forever. Stand, or be devoured.*

The air cracked. The Black Dragon emerged again, not as a phantom, but fully—armor as black as void, helm shaped like the skull of some ancient beast. His sword, jagged and cruel, dripped liquid shadow that hissed when it touched the ground.

"You cannot hide from me," he hissed. "Your flame belongs in chains."

The clash was instant.

He struck, a sweep of his blade that tore the earth itself open. Kaelen threw himself aside, rolling across broken stone. Lysera slammed her staff down, summoning a wall of vine and root glowing faint green—only for the Black Dragon's sword to cleave through it as if it were smoke.

Darek darted in from the side, daggers flashing. His blades struck gaps in the general's armor, but each hit dissolved into shadow. The knight turned and struck back with speed unnatural for his size. Darek barely leapt clear, a gash opening across his cloak.

"Steel won't touch him!" Darek spat.

Kaelen raised his hand, the blue flame surging brighter than before. He hurled it forward, a bolt of pure light that struck the Black Dragon square in the chest. For the first time, the knight staggered, shadows recoiling with a hiss.

The red eyes narrowed. "So the fox dares to bleed into you." His voice was venom. "Then I will carve her out."

The shadows thickened, flooding the ground. From them rose twisted forms: mirror-images of Kaelen, Lysera, and Darek, each made of smoke and hate. The illusions attacked, blades and staff and flame turned against them.

Kaelen clashed with his own shadow-self, its flame cold and hungry. Every strike echoed with his doubts: *You're too weak. You'll only fail as she did.*

Lysera's double lashed out with vines that strangled, hissing accusations: *You heal nothing. You are nothing.*

Darek's phantom sneered as it fought him blow for blow: *You always betray. You always will.*

The fox's voice cut through, sharp and urgent. *The flame is not a weapon. It is defiance. Endure.*

Kaelen clenched his fist. "We are not shadows!" he shouted. The flame burst outward, washing across the illusions. They shrieked, dissolving into smoke.

The Black Dragon recoiled again, snarling, his armor steaming where the light had touched.

But the effort drained Kaelen. His knees buckled. The flame dimmed.

The general raised his sword, shadows boiling. "Then you will fall in her place."

At the last instant, Lysera struck. She planted her staff into the ground, vines bursting upward, lashing around the general's arms and blade. Darek dove in, slamming both daggers into the cracks between the armor's plates where the blue flame had burned it. The general roared, staggering back, tearing the vines apart with sheer force.

"Now!" Lysera shouted.

Kaelen forced the last of his strength into the flame. It leapt from his hand, blindingly bright, striking the Black Dragon full in the chest. For a heartbeat, the knight's form fractured, his shadows peeling away like smoke caught in wind.

He reeled, his voice a growl that shook the earth. "This is not the end. You cannot run from me. I am the dark between breaths. I am the hunter, and you are prey."

And then his form collapsed into mist, vanishing into the night.

Silence fell, broken only by their ragged breathing.

Lysera leaned on her staff, pale and trembling. "We... drove him back."

"Not beaten," Darek said, though even his voice was shaken. "But we lived. That's more than most."

Kaelen stared at his hand, the flame flickering low. He felt Serenya's whisper stir, soft and resolute:

You cannot defeat him yet. But you can endure. And in enduring, you will grow stronger.

Kaelen closed his fist around the dying flame and whispered, "Then we'll endure."

Chapter Fifteen

The Scholar's Path

In Knowledge, the Flame Finds Shape

The dawn was pale, almost colorless, as it bled across the wastelands. Smoke still lingered from the night's battle, curling upward like fading fingers.

The three companions sat in silence, too weary to speak. Kaelen's flame flickered weakly in his hand, a reminder that though they had survived, they had not won.

At last, Lysera broke the silence. Her voice was hoarse, but steady. "We cannot keep fighting like this. Every step we take, another general will rise to stop us. Strength alone will not be enough."

Darek leaned back against a stone, one blade still resting across his knees. "She's right. The dragon last night—" he paused, his mouth tightening, "—he played with us. If he truly wanted us dead, we'd be bones in the dirt."

Kaelen clenched his fist around the shard they had taken. Its red glow pulsed faintly, held at bay by his flame. "Then what do we do?"

Lysera's gaze lifted to the horizon. "We find someone who understands this. The Stone. The fox. The Order. We fight blind, and that's why we're weak."

Darek gave a dry laugh. "And where do you expect to find someone who knows the secrets of the multiverse? Scholars don't exactly survive long under dragon rule."

But Lysera shook her head. "There are whispers. A scholar who still keeps the old records. A wanderer who hides among ruins, gathering fragments of history even the Draconis fear to burn. If he lives, he is our best chance."

Kaelen met her gaze. "You've heard of him?"

She nodded. "Only rumors. They call him **The Lorekeeper of Kalvasar.**"

At the name, Darek raised a brow. "Kalvasar's dead. Burned years ago."

"Not completely," Lysera said softly. "Some say beneath its ruins, the Lorekeeper tends a hidden library, protected by wards older than the Order itself. If anyone can tell us how to turn these shards into more than cursed trinkets, it's him."

Kaelen looked down at the shard in his hand, then at the weak flame in his palm. The fox's whisper touched him faintly, no louder than a breath:

Knowledge is a weapon the shadows cannot twist. Seek it.

He nodded slowly. "Then we go to Kalvasar."

Darek sheathed his blades with a resigned sigh. "I should've known I was signing up for more than petty thieving. Fine. I'll guide you through the ruins—if the place even exists anymore. But if your Lorekeeper turns out to be just another ghost story, don't say I didn't warn you."

Lysera's staff glowed faintly, its runes pulsing with determination. "Then it's settled. The road ahead will be worse than anything we've faced. But if knowledge is the key to fighting the generals, we must take it."

Kaelen tightened his grip on the shard. "Then Kalvasar it is."

The three stood, weary but resolute, the ruined horizon stretching before them. Somewhere beneath those shattered lands, truth awaited—and perhaps, the key to turning sparks of defiance into a flame strong enough to challenge dragons.

And high above, unseen, the Black Dragon lingered in the clouds of shadow, watching.

His laughter was a whisper in the wind.

Chapter Sixteen

The Taste of Defiance

The First Taste of Freedom's Fire

T he Obsidian Spire loomed eternal, its halls steeped in shadow and fire. Within its council chamber, the generals gathered once more, their thrones ringing the pulsing shards of the shattered **Eclipsera Stone**.

The air was tense.

The **Black Dragon** stood at the center, his armor cracked faintly where Kaelen's flame had struck. Though his presence was cold as void, the faint wound radiated humiliation.

"I hunted them," he said, his voice low and bitter. "The flame was weak. Their bodies fragile. Yet the fox's light shielded them." His helm tilted, eyes glowing like coals. "They endure."

The **Red Dragon** let out a guttural laugh that shook the chamber. "So the master of shadows returns, empty-handed. Tell me, hunter—did the prey bite back?"

The Black Dragon's gauntlet flexed, shadows writhing at his feet. "Mock me if you wish. But you did worse. At least I left them trembling in the dark. You let them steal a shard."

The Red Dragon rose with a snarl, fire spilling from his armor. But before the clash could ignite, Avarith's voice silenced them both.

"Enough."

The Dark Lord's gaze swept over his generals. His presence alone bent the chamber into silence.

"They live," Avarith said slowly, "and that means they matter. Not because they are strong, but because they have survived where others did not. Each time they endure, their spark grows brighter."

The **Azure Dragon** leaned forward, his armor shimmering like liquid sapphire. "Then why allow them to continue? Send us all. Snuff them out before they gather more strength."

But Avarith shook his head. "No. Fear must spread wider than fire. Let mortals see these sparks flicker, let them dare to hope—and then we shall smother it. Hope slain is more powerful than hope denied."

The **Silver Dragon** chuckled, his voice like a blade of ice. "So we bleed them slowly. How delicious."

Avarith's helm tilted, his ember-eyes narrowing. "But not too slowly. Black, you will follow them still, unseen. Red, your flames will await their return to the surface. And when the time is right..." His hand lifted, the shards of the Eclipsera Stone pulsing in unison. "...they will be broken, body and spirit. The fox will watch their corpses fall before her crystal prison."

The generals bowed, though some with fury in their eyes, others with hunger, and one—perhaps—with the faintest trace of doubt.

The hunt was not over.

It had only sharpened its claws.

Chapter Seventeen

The Fox's Oath

The Promise That Shadows Cannot Break

Within her crystal prison, Serenya shivered as the echoes of the Draconis council faded. She could not see the Obsidian Spire, nor the generals gathered around the fractured Stone—but the shards linked them all, and through those links, their words poisoned the silence around her.

Hope slain is more powerful than hope denied.
She will watch their corpses fall before her crystal prison.

The cruelty of it gnawed at her spirit. Every word was a blade twisting deeper, reminding her of her failure, of the day she had fallen. Once she had been a warrior whose light stretched across countless realms. Now she was nothing more than a fox bound in crystal, forced to watch while others bled in her place.

The shadows pressed closer, whispering Avarith's truth: *You are powerless. You can do nothing. You failed them once; you will fail them again.*

For a moment, Serenya's fire dimmed. She bowed her head, tails curling around her small form. The despair was suffocating.

But then—through the fractures of her prison—she felt it.

Kaelen's defiance, even as the Black Dragon towered above him.
Lysera's resolve, her staff driving roots into the dark.
Darek's sharp grin, refusing to yield even when outmatched.

They endured. *For her.*

Her eyes opened, burning bright blue once more.

"No," she whispered into the void. Her voice was faint, but steady. "I will not watch them die. Not again. If the only weapon I have is my voice, then I will wield it until the crystal itself shatters."

The crystal pulsed, cracks of light spidering faintly across its surface. Not enough to break it, but enough to ripple across the dream-currents like thunder.

She raised her head high, her fox-shape glowing brighter against the dark.

"You will not have them, Avarith. They are more than prey. They are the storm your order cannot contain. And I will guide them—until my prison is dust, until the Stone is whole, until balance sings again."

The shadows hissed, recoiling at her defiance. The prison still held, but for the first time, Serenya felt it weaken—not by force, but by *will.*

And in the distant wastelands, Kaelen stirred from uneasy sleep, feeling her whisper cut through his dreams:

"I am with you. Always."

Chapter Eighteen

The Dream of Ash and Flame

In Dreams, the Flame Remembers

T hat night, Kaelen did not sleep in peace.

The flame in his hand burned faintly as his body rested, and his mind was pulled into a place that was neither memory nor dream. A vast field of stars stretched above him, but half the heavens were veiled in shadow. The earth beneath his feet cracked with fire and bloom both, like two worlds colliding.

And in the midst of it stood the fox.

Her sapphire form glowed softly, her tails curling like wisps of starlight. Her voice, when it came, was steady and sorrowful, yet strong enough to shake the void:

"I must show you what lies ahead. Not to bind you—but to remind you why you must endure."

The stars twisted.

The Vision of Failure

Kaelen saw himself and his companions in ruins deeper than any they had yet faced. Lysera lay broken, her staff splintered, vines withered. Darek was on his knees, his daggers fallen, his eyes empty with betrayal.

And above them, the Draconis Order stood triumphant. The Red Dragon's fire scorched their bodies. The Black Dragon's shadow drowned their last light. Avarith himself raised the Eclipsera Stone, fully whole but corrupted, its light bled into crimson.

In the crystal nearby, Serenya screamed soundlessly, forced to watch as Kaelen fell. The flame in his hand flickered out.

The dream-world shuddered with despair.

"This is what awaits if you falter," her whisper said, trembling but clear. *"This is the silence of unbroken chains."*

The Vision of Triumph

The darkness shattered, and the stars blazed anew. Kaelen saw himself standing not as a farmer's son, but as a warrior, the flame in his hand now a blazing sword of blue light. Lysera stood at his side, her staff flowering with emerald fire, roots binding even the sky. Darek moved in the shadows, striking like lightning, his grin sharp with defiance.

And beside them, no longer bound in fox-shape, stood Serenya herself—armor of dawn and dusk restored, her blade of cosmic fire lifted high.

Together, they faced the Draconis generals. And one by one, the dragons fell, their stolen shards returning to the Stone until it shone whole again. The universes mended. Balance sang once more.

"And this," her whisper softened, *"is what may yet come, if you endure. Not because you were chosen, but because you chose to rise."*

Kaelen dropped to his knees, overwhelmed. "Why me? I'm no warrior. I'm no leader. I'm just—"

The fox's eyes glowed, her voice cutting through his doubt:

"So was I, once."

The dream dissolved.

Kaelen awoke in the ruins with tears on his face, his hand clenched tight around the shard and the flame both. He did not speak, but when Lysera stirred at his side and Darek raised a brow in silence, Kaelen only said:

"We keep going. We *have* to."

The fox's whisper lingered in his chest, faint but unwavering:

"You carry both ruin and salvation in your hands. Choose the flame. Always the flame."

Chapter Nineteen

The Long Road of Ash

Through Ash, the Path Endures

T he journey to Kalvasar was no path but a wound across the
world.

For weeks they walked through wastelands stripped bare by dragonfire. The skies above bled gray and red, clouds cracked by the glow
of molten rivers. Carcasses of once-great forests stood as blackened
husks, their twisted branches clawing the air like the dead. Cities lay
scattered as skeletons of stone, their towers leaning into the dirt as if
bowing to despair.

Every step reminded them of what had been lost.

And every step tested their bond.

Kaelen's Burden

Kaelen carried the shard, its sickly pulse constantly gnawing at him. The flame in his hand pushed back its corruption, but the effort left him weary, his skin pale, his eyes shadowed. Sometimes, in the dead of night, he swore he heard voices whispering from the shard itself—temptations of power, promises that if he gave in, he could burn the Draconis where they stood.

But each time, he tightened his grip and remembered Serenya's whisper: *"Choose the flame. Always the flame."*

Lysera often sat near him, her staff humming softly, weaving healing light around him when the shard's corruption grew strongest. Her quiet presence steadied him more than words could.

Lysera's Strength

It was Lysera who kept them alive on the road. She found water where none should be, coaxed roots to sprout from dead ground, and mended wounds both seen and unseen. But the further they went, the more her body paid the cost. Every spell drained her, every day left her weaker.

Kaelen tried to help, fumbling with her runes, but it was Darek who surprised them most. He carried water without complaint, sharpened her staff's iron bands against rust, and once, when she nearly collapsed, caught her without a word and set her down with surprising gentleness.

When she thanked him, he only smirked. "Don't mention it. Ever."

Darek's Shadows

For all his sharp tongue and mocking grin, Darek began to reveal pieces of himself. At night, by dying campfires, he told half-jokes about his past—robbing Draconis caravans, tricking patrols into chasing shadows. But sometimes his words trailed into silence, and his eyes grew distant, haunted by ghosts he did not name.

One night, when Kaelen asked why he stayed with them, Darek shrugged. "Maybe I'm tired of running alone. Or maybe I want to see if sparks can really light a fire." His grin was sharp, but there was no mockery in it.

The Road of Trials

The wastelands themselves became their enemy.

Ash storms scoured their skin raw, forcing them to cling to each other for shelter. Once, they crossed the bones of a fallen titan-beast, its ribcage forming a valley where echoes of its death screamed on the wind. Another time, they stumbled into a canyon where shadows clung unnaturally thick—remnants of the Black Dragon's passing. Kaelen's flame was the only thing that led them out.

Each trial bound them closer, their trust forged in hardship.

At last, after days that felt like years, the ruins of **Kalvasar** rose on the horizon.

The once-great city was a grave of stone and fire. Towers split in half like broken teeth. Bridges collapsed into black rivers. Ash hung so thick that the sun barely pierced it.

But beneath the ruin, they could feel something stirring. Knowledge. Secrets. Perhaps... hope.

Kaelen clenched the shard in his palm, the flame burning steady. Lysera's eyes narrowed with determination. Darek's grin flickered, nervous but unyielding.

Together, they stepped toward the broken gates of Kalvasar.

And deep within her crystal, Serenya whispered with fierce resolve: *"Find him. The Lorekeeper waits."*

Chapter Twenty

Echoes of Kalvasar

The Ash of Yesterday Still Speaks

The gates of **Kalvasar** loomed like the jaws of a dead beast. Blackened stone, carved once with flowing runes of light, now lay cracked and crumbling, their inscriptions burned into illegibility. The city stretched inward like a corpse, streets hollowed by fire, towers leaning like broken spears, and silence clinging like a shroud.

Yet beneath that silence... something moved.

The Streets of Ash

As Kaelen, Lysera, and Darek stepped through the shattered archway, the weight of the ruin pressed down. The air itself carried whispers, faint echoes of laughter, prayer, and life that had long since burned away. Their footsteps stirred ash that once might have been flowers, or books, or even bodies.

Kaelen gripped the shard beneath his cloak. It pulsed faintly, almost eagerly, as if the corruption remembered this place. His flame flared in answer, struggling to suppress it.

"This city..." Lysera whispered, her voice hushed in reverence and grief. "I studied its lore as a child. Kalvasar was said to be the greatest treasury of knowledge in the worlds. Its libraries were vast enough to drown in. Now..." Her words faltered. "Now it is a tomb."

Darek scanned the shadows warily, blades loose in his hands. "And like any tomb, it's bound to have things crawling that shouldn't."

The First Trap

As they moved deeper, the silence cracked. A low hum began to reverberate across the streets, echoing like a heartbeat. The stones beneath their feet shifted—then split open.

Glyphs long-buried flared to life, ancient wards crafted not against dragons, but thieves. Runes of defense, corrupted by time, twisted and wild.

From the cracks surged spectral guardians—figures of pale blue light clad in crumbling armor, faces erased by time. Their weapons shimmered with the same energy, echoing fragments of the city's last defenders.

"They're... memories," Lysera gasped. "Shadows of Kalvasar's fallen."

But the guardians did not recognize friend from foe. Their hollow eyes locked onto the intruders.

"They don't care who we are," Darek muttered, blades flashing. "They'll cut us down all the same!"

Haunted Battle

The fight was chaos. The spectral soldiers moved with unnatural precision, blades passing through stone yet cutting flesh like steel. Kaelen's flame flared, clashing with their energy, driving some back, though the shard in his hand trembled as if hungering for them.

Lysera raised her staff, runes blazing green, her vines wrapping spectral blades in futile grasps before bursting into flame. Each spell drained her further, sweat pouring down her brow.

Darek danced through the ruins with shadows and steel, striking at weak points where the light flickered, cutting down one after another—but for each that fell, two more rose from the streets.

"They won't stop!" Kaelen shouted, his chest heaving.

Lysera's eyes widened with sudden realization. "The wards—they're self-sustaining! We can't fight them. We have to *break the runes*!"

Kaelen looked around wildly. Faint glyphs still glowed along the walls and the cobbled street, their ancient script pulsing with corrupted rhythm.

"Then show me where!" he cried.

Breaking the Past

Guided by Lysera's knowledge, Kaelen thrust the blue flame into the runes themselves. Each time, the glyph shrieked as though alive, the light exploding in sparks. The guardians faltered when one rune collapsed, then flickered violently as another fell.

Darek leapt onto a half-fallen column, shattering a glowing crest with his blade. Lysera slammed her staff into another, vines pulling stone apart to break its seal.

At last, Kaelen thrust his flame into the largest rune—etched across a wall like a bleeding scar. With a roar of light, it shattered.

The guardians froze, their weapons raised—then crumbled into dust, dissolving back into silence.

The streets were still again.

The Deeper City

The trio stood panting amid the ruin, sweat streaking their ash-smeared faces.

Kaelen clenched the shard tighter, his flame still burning faint. "If this is the *outer* city..." he muttered, "what waits deeper in?"

Lysera looked toward the city's heart, where the blackened spires of the central library pierced the sky. Her expression was grim, but resolute.

"Knowledge," she said. "And knowledge is never unguarded."

Darek gave a low whistle, sheathing his blades. "Well then, let's hope this Lorekeeper knows how to make an entrance worth all this trouble."

Together, they pressed forward, deeper into Kalvasar's haunted bones—toward secrets that might save the multiverse... or damn it further.

And unseen, in the ruins' highest tower, a single lantern flickered to life. A watcher. A presence. Someone who had expected them.

Chapter
Twenty-One

The City That Remembers

The Walls Speak What Time Cannot Silence

T he silence after the collapse of the spectral guardians did not last long.

Kalvasar was a city that had died screaming, and even in ruin, it remembered.

The Streets of Memory

As they pressed further inward, the air grew heavier. The ash that had lain quiet on the ground stirred as if to watch them. Faint whispers bled through the walls of collapsed homes—snatches of laughter, prayers, and pleas that had been carved into the stone itself, now looping endlessly.

Kaelen felt them brushing his mind like claws. At first they were only echoes, but soon they became *voices*. His father's, telling him he should never have survived when so many stronger had burned. His mother's, begging him not to leave her a second time.

He staggered, clutching his head.

Lysera's hand caught his shoulder, her staff glowing faintly to push the whispers back. "The city was sealed in fire," she murmured. "Its death was etched into its stones. You're not hearing the dead—you're hearing their pain."

Darek spat, glaring at the walls. "Then let's move before their pain drowns us all."

The Illusionary Market

They turned a corner and found themselves in what had once been a marketplace. To their shock, it was still whole—stalls lined with fruit, merchants laughing, children weaving through the crowd.

"It's…" Kaelen whispered, "alive?"

But Lysera's eyes hardened. "No. Look closer."

The illusion faltered at its edges, flickering like a frayed tapestry. Beneath the smiles, faces twisted, mouths opening to reveal fire where teeth should be. The children turned, their eyes hollow, and the laughter warped into screams.

The market collapsed into flame, and the ground itself split. The trio barely leapt aside as the cobbles melted into molten pits.

"This city doesn't want us here," Darek growled, blades drawn. "It's trying to kill us."

Lysera shook her head grimly. "Not the city. The corruption. The Draconis burned Kalvasar so completely that even its memories rot."

The Corridor of Hands

They fled the collapsing market and stumbled into an alley. Here, walls jutted close, forcing them into single file. The air grew thick and suffocating.

Then the walls began to move.

From the stone stretched *hands*—charred, broken, spectral—reaching for them. At first they clawed weakly, but then they grasped with strength enough to drag.

One seized Kaelen's arm, pulling him toward the wall as if to swallow him whole. He cried out, the flame in his hand bursting to life and searing it away. Lysera's staff lashed out with runes that burst like flares, while Darek's daggers hacked at stone that bled shadow.

They fought their way through, every step a battle, until at last the alley opened into a square. The hands retracted, vanishing into silence.

Kaelen bent double, gasping. His palm burned, the flame guttering. "This place... wants us broken."

Lysera placed a hand on his shoulder. "Then we'll break it first."

The Library in Ash

They stood now before the broken heart of Kalvasar—the Grand Archive.

Its spires leaned but still stood, their shattered windows glowing faintly with a sickly red light. The doors were half-collapsed, carved with runes once meant to protect knowledge from decay. Now those runes pulsed with corruption, like veins of blood across stone.

Darek gave a low whistle. "If your Lorekeeper lives in there, he's either the bravest man alive... or the most insane."

Lysera's eyes shone with grim awe. "Both, perhaps."

Kaelen tightened his grip on the shard, feeling it pulse in answer to the runes. "Then we go in."

And as they stepped toward the Archive, unseen eyes followed them from the shadows of the broken towers—measuring their courage, and their worth.

Chapter Twenty-Two

The Grand Archive

In Silence, the Pages Whisper

The doors of the Archive groaned as they pushed against them, a sound like bones breaking. Ash spilled from the cracks, and with it a wave of stale heat—air that had not been disturbed in years.

Inside, the **Grand Archive** was a cathedral of ruin.

Towers of shelves stretched high, their wood blackened, scrolls and tomes rotting in place. Where once there had been a sanctuary of knowledge, now corruption crept like ivy. Runes glowed faintly across the floor, twisted red, pulsing like veins of a diseased heart.

And in the silence, the books whispered.

Not with words, but with fragments: voices layered atop one another, fragments of knowledge, spells, histories—all shattered and overlapping until they became a ceaseless murmur, like a crowd of ghosts.

Kaelen shivered. "It feels... alive."

Lysera's face was pale but reverent. "It remembers. Kalvasar was the mind of the worlds. And now it is fractured. Every book, every record, every soul who wrote them—burned, bound, twisted into this."

Darek grimaced, blades half-drawn. "If this is the mind of the worlds, then the worlds went mad a long time ago."

The First Descent

They pressed deeper into the Archive. The shelves leaned like giants, their shadows forming cages. The floor was cracked, opening into pits where molten light glowed faintly. At times, words would burst from the walls—scribbled in flame across stone, only to fade as quickly as they appeared.

One corridor ended in a massive mural, once painted with constellations. Now it writhed, the stars twisting into the shape of dragon heads.

Kaelen reached out instinctively, but the fox's whisper stopped him. *Do not touch what the Order has corrupted.*

They turned instead into the **central atrium**, where a vast dome loomed overhead. Half the ceiling had collapsed, but enough remained to show mosaics of universes turning in harmony, all linked by the glow of a radiant stone.

The Eclipsera.

Even blackened by time, its image still burned in Kaelen's chest.

The Guardian of Ink and Ash

A sudden *crash* split the silence. One of the shelves groaned, then toppled, collapsing into the atrium. From the rubble poured not dust, but **ink**—thick, black, and writhing.

The ink pulled itself upward, shaping into a towering figure: a librarian's robe shredded into tendrils, its face blank parchment smeared with letters that twisted and crawled. Its hands were quills sharpened into claws.

The Archive had birthed a guardian of its own decay.

It screamed without a mouth, the sound like pages tearing.

"Of course it's alive," Darek muttered grimly, blades drawn. "Why wouldn't it be?"

The guardian lunged.

The Fight in the Atrium

Kaelen hurled his flame forward, the blue fire burning the ink where it touched. The creature shrieked, recoiling, but every drop of ink that fell from it crawled across the ground, reforming into more claws.

Lysera slammed her staff into the floor, summoning roots that burst through cracked stone to bind the tendrils. But the ink seeped up the vines, corrupting them black, forcing her to burn her own magic away before it reached her.

Darek moved like lightning, slashing tendrils apart, dodging swipes that could have torn him in half. His daggers cut through parchment-flesh, but the guardian simply reknit itself, letters scrambling to close the wounds.

"It won't stop!" Kaelen shouted.

Lysera's eyes locked on the runes burning across the atrium floor. "It's bound here—anchored to the corruption! Break the runes!"

Kaelen nodded, thrusting his flame downward into the glowing symbols. Each one he shattered weakened the guardian, its body flickering and faltering. Darek cut down tendrils faster than they could reform, buying him time, while Lysera poured her strength into holding the roots in place.

At last, Kaelen struck the central rune. The flame roared, and the ink guardian shrieked as its body collapsed into black rain that sizzled into nothingness.

The whispers of the books quieted—for a moment.

The Stairs Below

The atrium fell silent again. The trio stood among ruined shelves, breathing hard.

Then, from behind the shattered mural of the Eclipsera, stone shifted. A hidden stair groaned open, spiraling downward into darkness.

Kaelen tightened his grip on the shard and the flame.

Darek wiped his blades clean, smirking despite the ash on his face. "Well. Either that's the way to your Lorekeeper... or straight to the abyss."

Lysera's eyes glowed faintly green, determination carved into her features. "Knowledge always lies deeper."

They descended into the dark.

And far below, in chambers untouched by centuries, a single lantern waited.

Chapter
Twenty-Three

The Hidden Stairs

Steps Carved in Silence

The stairwell yawned before them, spiraling into darkness. Its steps were carved of blackened stone, smooth with age but veined with glowing cracks of red. Faint whispers drifted up from below, not like the murmurs of the books above, but deeper, older — the kind of voices that spoke from beneath the weight of centuries.

Kaelen tightened his grip on the flame, its glow pushing back the gloom. Darek smirked uneasily. "Down we go then, into the mouth of the abyss."

Lysera's staff glowed with runes of pale green, steady against the oppressive dark. "If the Lorekeeper survives, this is where he waits. But beware... if knowledge is preserved here, so too are the things meant to guard it."

They descended.

The Descent

The air grew colder the deeper they went, heavy with dust and the faint metallic tang of old blood. The walls were carved with faded runes — not of corruption, but of preservation. Some still pulsed faintly, struggling to endure despite the weight of time.

At intervals, they passed niches in the wall, where skeletal remains sat in ancient robes. Each figure clutched a book pressed against its chest, as though even in death they had refused to let go of their knowledge.

Darek glanced at them uneasily. "Charming. A library of corpses."

Lysera bowed her head in respect. "Archivists. They died keeping the knowledge safe, even as the city burned. Their vigil never ended."

Kaelen felt a pang of awe. To die for knowledge — not for survival, not for glory, but to protect truth. It humbled him.

The Chamber of Mirrors

At last the stairs ended, opening into a vast chamber. Here, the walls were not stone but polished obsidian, reflecting their forms in ghostly distortion. The ceiling stretched into shadow, but hanging lanterns flickered faintly, casting ripples of dim light across the mirrors.

As they stepped inside, their reflections *moved*.

Kaelen froze as he watched his mirrored self raise the shard in its hand, but instead of a steady flame, it was engulfed in shadow, eyes glowing crimson. Lysera's reflection showed her robes torn, vines twisted black, her face pale with corruption. Darek's mirror-image turned its blades not against enemies, but against his companions.

"They're lies," Lysera whispered, clutching her staff. "Twists of what could be."

But the reflections did not stay in the glass. One by one, they stepped free, their forms solidifying into flesh and steel.

"Wonderful," Darek muttered, blades flashing into his hands. "Now we get to fight ourselves."

The Battle With Their Doubles

The fight was brutal. Each mirrored double fought with their own strengths — Kaelen's reflection hurled dark flame, forcing him to counter with his true light. Lysera's shadow-self lashed out with vines that strangled, forcing her to burn her own magic brighter to resist. Darek's double fought with perfect mimicry, predicting every strike, every feint, forcing him into desperate improvisation.

Kaelen was driven to his knees, his flame sputtering as his reflection pressed close. "This is what you will become," the dark Kaelen hissed. "Weakness leads only to corruption."

But Serenya's whisper cut through, sharp as a blade: *"You are not your shadow. You are the choice to endure it."*

With a roar, Kaelen thrust his flame outward. His double shrieked, dissolving into shards of light. The others followed suit — Lysera's staff burned her reflection to ash, while Darek's unorthodox strike —

headbutting his double before stabbing both blades through its chest — sent it collapsing into smoke.

The chamber fell silent.

Their reflections were gone.

But the path forward had revealed itself — a door at the far end of the mirror hall, carved with ancient wards, faint light glowing from beyond its cracks.

The Threshold of the Lorekeeper

The three stood before it, weary but unbroken.

Kaelen's flame steadied in his palm. Lysera raised her staff, runes humming. Darek rolled his shoulders with a wry grin.

"Well," he said, "if the man behind this door isn't your Lorekeeper, then he had better be something worse — because I'm not leaving without answers."

Together, they pushed the door open.

And within the chamber beyond, a single lantern burned — beside the figure of an old man seated at a desk of stone, surrounded by books that had somehow survived the fall of Kalvasar. His eyes, sharp as fire and shadow both, lifted to meet theirs.

"I wondered when you would arrive," the Lorekeeper said.

Chapter Twenty-Four

The Lorekeeper of Kalvasar

Guardian of Forgotten Truths

The chamber was unlike the ruin above. Where the city had burned, this place had endured. The walls were smooth stone etched with faint, ancient wards that glowed dimly, holding back the corruption. Stacks of books, scrolls, and tablets lined the room in careful order, though many were cracked with age.

At the center sat an old man. His hair was silver-white, long but well-kept, his robes patched yet dignified. His eyes were deep and sharp, shifting like candlelight—one moment warm, the next burning with something unreadable.

A lantern burned at his desk, steady despite the suffocating air.

When he spoke, his voice was quiet, but carried with it the weight of centuries.

"I wondered when you would arrive," he said, not looking surprised, as though he had expected them. "The fox's whispers are not easily hidden, even from one such as I."

First Impressions

Kaelen froze, flame trembling in his hand. "You... know of her?"

The Lorekeeper's gaze turned to him, piercing. "I know of many things, boy. I know of stones that bind worlds together, of warriors who fell when they should have stood, and of children who carry burdens far heavier than they deserve. You are not the first the fox has called. But perhaps..." His eyes narrowed. "...you may be the first to reach me alive."

Lysera bowed slightly, her staff glowing faintly. "You are the Lorekeeper of Kalvasar?"

A faint smile ghosted the old man's lips. "That is what they call me. But names matter little. I am the last of those who swore to guard what knowledge the Order could not burn. The mind of the worlds was fractured when Kalvasar fell. I tend what fragments remain."

Darek crossed his arms, skeptical. "If you've been hiding down here all this time, why didn't you stop them? Why let the Draconis take everything?"

The Lorekeeper's eyes hardened. "Because knowledge is not a sword to swing at dragons. Knowledge endures. It waits until those who can wield it arrive."

The First Truths of the Stone

The old man leaned back, studying the shard Kaelen carried. Its sickly red glow pulsed against the blue flame surrounding it.

"That," he said softly, "is both your greatest weapon and your greatest curse. A shard of the **Eclipsera Stone**, torn from the heart of balance by Avarith and his Order. In its wholeness, it sang harmony across the universes. In its shattering, it screams."

Kaelen's hand trembled. "It tries to corrupt me. Whisper things. Promise me power."

The Lorekeeper nodded gravely. "Of course. Each shard remembers the hand of the general who claimed it. That one..." His eyes flickered with recognition. "The Red Dragon's. Fire and ruin. It will forever hunger to burn, even as your flame resists it. But so long as you guard it, the shard cannot consume you."

Lysera leaned forward, eyes sharp. "Then if we reclaim them all, if we make the Stone whole again..."

"Balance may return," the Lorekeeper said, his voice laced with both hope and warning. "Or it may break the worlds entirely. The Stone was not meant to be shattered. To reforge it is to gamble with existence itself."

Cryptic Counsel

Silence hung heavy.

Kaelen's chest tightened. "Then what are we supposed to do? We can't fight generals like the Black Dragon—not as we are. We barely survived him."

The Lorekeeper's eyes gleamed. "And yet you did. That is no small thing." He rose slowly, his movements deliberate, as though each gesture carried meaning. He placed a hand on a nearby tome, its cover bound in starlight thread.

"Knowledge cannot fight in your place. But it can *guide*. Each general wears more than armor—they wear the echoes of the Stone's power they stole. To fight them, you must understand not only their strengths, but their *flaws*. Every shadow has a root, every flame a weakness."

He studied them in silence for a long moment, then spoke with gravity.

"If you are to reclaim what was lost, you must walk three paths: endure the flame, resist the shadow, and seek the truth buried beneath lies. Only then will you stand before Avarith and not fall as she did."

Kaelen's flame flickered in his hand, steadier now. Serenya's whisper stirred faintly through him, warm with hope:

"At last... someone who remembers."

Chapter Twenty-Five

The Weakness of Flame

Where Light Flickers, Shadows Press Close

The Lorekeeper moved slowly through the chamber, lantern-light flickering across his lined face. His hand brushed over scrolls and tomes as though each carried a memory. When he stopped, it was before a great tablet, cracked but still legible, etched with runes that glowed faintly.

He turned to them, his eyes steady.

"You ask for truth, and truth I will give. But know this—truth is both weapon and burden. To learn the flaws of a dragon is to take on the duty of striking when none else can."

Kaelen's jaw tightened, but he nodded. "We need to know. If we don't, we'll fall the next time we face them."

The old man studied him for a long moment, then spoke.

The Red Dragon's Hunger

"The Red Dragon," the Lorekeeper began, "is fire unchained. His armor is forged from the heart of a dead star, and his axe drinks the lifeblood of every world he burns. He is destruction made flesh. You have felt his power already."

Kaelen shivered, remembering the molten ground, the way the air itself had screamed.

"But fire," the Lorekeeper said softly, "is not infinite. It is a hunger. It must feed. And therein lies his weakness."

Lysera leaned forward, eyes sharp. "What do you mean?"

The Lorekeeper tapped the tablet. "The Red Dragon cannot conjure flame from nothing. He draws it from the world around him. Every battle he wages weakens the land itself—burning stone, air, and soul. When the land is barren, his power falters. When he starves, his flames become desperation, wild and unfocused."

Kaelen's flame flickered in his hand. "So if we can endure him long enough... he burns himself out?"

"Not easily," the Lorekeeper said gravely. "For even a dying fire may consume all before it fades. But yes—endure, and he will falter. Turn his hunger against him, and you may yet see him fall."

The Warning of Shadows

He stepped closer, his gaze darkening. "But do not mistake one truth for all truths. Each general is different. The Black Dragon you faced? His strength is not hunger, but fear. The Azure weaves illusions sharper than blades. Each flaw is hidden in their nature, and only knowledge can unearth it."

He leaned over the desk, eyes narrowing.

"You must decide what you are willing to sacrifice to exploit these flaws. Endurance demands pain. Illusions demand clarity. Shadows demand courage. Every path you walk will scar you."

The Burden of Knowledge

Silence lingered in the chamber as the trio absorbed his words.

Darek let out a low whistle. "So our grand plan is to starve a dragon of fire. Simple." His grin was thin. "Guess that means we'll be running for our lives again soon enough."

Lysera ignored him, her voice low but steady. "Thank you, Lorekeeper. With this knowledge, we may stand a chance."

The old man's eyes softened—just slightly. "Do not thank me yet. I give you weapons, yes. But I also give you chains. For now you cannot walk blind. You know his hunger. You must face it."

He leaned back, folding his hands.

"The fox chose you not for strength, but for the will to endure. Do not forget that. For endurance is the only fire that never dies."

Kaelen felt the shard in his hand pulse, and for the first time, the flame did not falter. It burned steady, defiant. Serenya's whisper echoed faintly:

"Now you begin to see."

Chapter Twenty-Six

The City's Last Trial

Balance Demands Its Price

The Lorekeeper's words still echoed in their minds as they turned to leave the chamber. The lantern-light behind him dimmed, though his eyes followed them, sharp as ever.

"You carry knowledge now," he said softly. "Guard it well. Kalvasar has given what it can... but it will also demand its price."

Kaelen's hand tightened around the shard, the flame in his palm flickering steady. "We'll endure it."

The old man only inclined his head, his expression unreadable. "Then go. The city will test you one last time."

The Rising Archive

The stairs they had descended were gone. In their place yawned a vast chasm, shelves rising from the depths like jagged teeth. Tomes fluttered from their places, their pages unraveling into tendrils of ink that reached for them.

Darek swore under his breath. "Of course the city doesn't want us to leave."

Lysera's runes flared bright, weaving protective light. "The corruption is rooted deepest here. It won't let its secrets go easily."

Kaelen stepped forward, his flame burning blue against the ink tendrils. Each lash recoiled, but more followed, the chasm filling with a writhing storm of pages and claws.

Flight Through the Ruins

They ran. Across collapsing bridges of stone, through shelves that toppled like towers, dodging claws of living script that carved the air. Kaelen's flame burned a path, Lysera's staff shielded them, and Darek's blades cut down tendrils before they could drag anyone away.

But the Archive fought back harder with every step. Illusions of scholars appeared, begging them to stay. Shadows whispered promises of knowledge greater than any dragon's power if only they turned back. The air itself grew heavy with voices that threatened to drown thought.

Kaelen's flame faltered under the weight of it—until Serenya's whisper steadied him. *"Do not linger in the past. Carry it forward."*

With renewed strength, he surged ahead, the flame blazing, burning the illusions into ash.

The Gate of Ash

At last, they reached the broken gates of Kalvasar. The city shuddered behind them, as if mourning its secrets. A final roar of collapsing stone echoed like thunder as the Grand Archive sealed itself forever, burying its horrors in the dark.

The three staggered into the wastelands, gasping for breath. The shard pulsed faintly, but Kaelen's flame held it steady.

Lysera lowered her staff, her voice weary but firm. "We have what we came for. Knowledge. A path forward."

Darek smirked, though it didn't quite reach his eyes. "And a dozen new nightmares to haunt my sleep."

Kaelen looked back once, the ruined spires of Kalvasar fading into the ash-stained horizon. He felt the weight of what they carried now—not only the shard, but the truth of the Red Dragon's hunger.

He clenched his fist. "Next time... we'll be ready."

And from her crystal, Serenya whispered with fierce pride:

"Yes. The storm grows stronger."

Chapter Twenty-Seven

The Generals' Fury

Wrath Unleashed, Shadows Unbound

The Obsidian Spire's chamber darkened as the shards of the Eclipsera Stone pulsed with agitation. From them, echoes stirred—faint ripples of knowledge carried through the broken harmony. The mortals had entered Kalvasar. Worse—they had left it alive.

The Red Dragon slammed his axe into the stone floor, sparks scattering. "Impossible! The Archive should have devoured them. Ink, illusion, memory—Kalvasar was a grave. Yet they crawl back from it, clutching truths that should have stayed buried!"

The Azure Dragon's voice slithered like liquid. "Then the whispers are true. The Lorekeeper still endures. Even flame could not erase him." His helm tilted, reflective scales shifting like waves. "If they reached him, then they carry more than shards now. They carry *knowledge.*"

The Black Dragon's armor seethed with shadow. His words were low, but heavy with venom. "Knowledge is more dangerous than any blade. They learned my weakness in the hunt. And now, perhaps, they know yours, Red."

The Red Dragon roared, fire bursting from his helm. "Let them try! Let the boy's spark stand against my inferno—he will be ash before he breathes twice."

But Avarith's hand lifted, silencing them all.

Avarith's Judgment

The Dark Lord rose from his throne, obsidian armor glowing with veins of molten fire. His gaze swept across his generals, and the weight of it pressed silence into the chamber.

"Do not underestimate them." His voice was iron, each word cutting deep. "They endure what should not be endured. First the hunt. Now the city of ghosts. The fox's light guides them still, and the Lorekeeper feeds their flame."

His helm tilted slightly, eyes glowing ember-red.

"Good."

The generals shifted uneasily.

"Good?" the Silver Dragon scoffed, his voice a dagger of arrogance. "You would let them grow?"

Avarith's laughter rumbled like distant thunder. "What is hope, if not a weapon we may turn against them? Let them cling to it. Let them gather their strength, their allies, their truths. Let them think themselves dangerous." His voice dropped into a hiss. "And then, when they burn brightest... we will snuff them out before all the worlds."

The Orders Given

He raised his hand, the shards of the Stone flaring.

"Black—watch them still. Let your shadow follow every step. Red—prepare your flame. Their endurance will falter when you starve them of land to stand on. Azure— weave illusions among the mortals, twist whispers of rebellion into fear. Let the spark they light burn their own people."

Each general bowed their head, some with fury, others with grim anticipation.

But as they departed, the chamber hummed with unspoken tension. For the first time, even among the Draconis, there was unease.

The prey had survived too much.

And somewhere deep in the crystal prison, Serenya felt their malice coil tighter. She whispered fiercely into the dream-currents:

"Hold fast. Their eyes are upon you now. But knowledge is your shield. Do not let their fear become your own."

Chapter Twenty-Eight

Hunger of the Wasteland

Nothing Endures but Hunger

The wastelands stretched endless before them—cracked earth, rivers of cooled ash, and skies the color of old blood. Kalvasar's silhouette had long since vanished behind the horizon, yet the weight of the Archive lingered heavy in their minds.

The shard pulsed faintly in Kaelen's hand, sickly red, but the flame wrapped around it held steady. Each beat of its hunger reminded him of the truth the Lorekeeper had given them:

The Red Dragon burns because he must feed. Fire is not endless. It consumes until nothing is left.

Testing the Truth

They traveled across a land once vibrant with life. Now it was dead—a wasteland scorched by dragonfire long ago. Nothing stirred but the wind. For days, not even a scavenger's shadow crossed their path.

And for days, Kaelen noticed something. His flame flickered less, the shard pulsed weaker.

He told Lysera one night as they camped beside the bones of a fallen tower. "The shard feels... hungry. But there's nothing left here to feed on. It's weaker."

Lysera nodded gravely. "Then the Lorekeeper was right. Even the dragons' power is tied to the world itself. When they strip it bare, they strip themselves too."

Darek gave a sharp laugh. "So what's our plan? March this Red bastard into the middle of a desert and wait for him to sputter out?"

Kaelen managed a faint smile. "Maybe."

Lysera's gaze softened, though her voice was firm. "If he falters in barren lands, then the wastelands are our ally. We must draw him where he cannot feed. And endure long enough to see him break."

Bonds on the Road

The journey was merciless. Sandstorms scoured their skin raw, and heat by day gave way to bitter cold by night. Their rations dwindled, and thirst gnawed at them as cruelly as the shard's pulse.

Yet in suffering, their bond deepened.

Lysera gave what strength she had to heal their wounds and coax bitter roots from poisoned soil, often leaving herself drained to exhaustion. Kaelen supported her without hesitation, carrying her staff when her arms faltered.

Darek scouted ahead tirelessly, his sharp eyes finding paths through shattered canyons. Once, when Kaelen collapsed from heat and the shard's pull, it was Darek who dragged him to shade, muttering, "Don't think I'm carrying you twice."

That night, though, he kept watch longer than either of them, eyes never leaving the horizon.

The Whisper of the Fox

One night, Kaelen dreamed again. Serenya's voice came through clearer than it had since Kalvasar:

"You begin to see. They cannot be met in strength. But weakness hides in hunger, fear, and pride. Each general bears their flaw as much as their power. Use it."

Her fox-shape glowed faintly in the dream, tails curling around him. Her eyes, though weary, burned with defiance.

"And remember—your endurance feeds mine. Every step you take weakens my chains. Do not falter."

Kaelen awoke with renewed fire.

Resolve

The next morning, as the wasteland stretched into another endless horizon, he spoke aloud what they all felt.

"The Red Dragon will come again. When he does—we don't have to beat him in fire. We just have to *outlast* him."

Lysera nodded, her staff glowing softly in approval.

Darek smirked, spinning a dagger in his hand. "Endurance. Not exactly my specialty. But if it means seeing a dragon choke on its own hunger? Count me in."

They pressed onward, battered but unbroken. And far above, unseen in the clouds, the Black Dragon's shadow followed still, watching, waiting.

Chapter
Twenty-Nine

The Hermit of Glass Dunes

In Solitude, the Desert Remembers

T he wastelands stretched unbroken for days. Ash gave way to sand, pale and sharp like shards of broken glass, scattered by winds that howled like beasts. Their rations were nearly gone, and the air shimmered with heat by day, freezing their bones by night.

It was here, in the *Glass Dunes*, that they found him.

The Stranger

At first, Kaelen thought it a mirage. A figure stood at the crest of a dune, robes tattered but moving with deliberate precision, as though the storms bent around him. His staff was longer than Lysera's, carved from crystal instead of wood, etched with lines that glowed faintly blue.

When the wind parted, they saw his face: an older man, scarred, his eyes hidden beneath a band of cloth. Yet even blind, his gaze felt piercing.

"Lost children," he said, his voice dry as the sands. "Carrying fire you do not yet understand."

Darek muttered, half under his breath, "Wonderful. Another cryptic old man in the middle of nowhere."

Lysera, though, stiffened. "I know of him. Or of his kind. A scholar-warrior of the Starward Order. They were keepers of the Stone's histories... before the Draconis burned them."

The stranger inclined his head. "Once, perhaps. Now I am only a hermit, waiting for the desert to claim me. Yet the fox whispers even here. She led you across my dunes."

A Test of Will

Before Kaelen could answer, the hermit lifted his staff. The sand rose with it, spiraling into shapes — blades, beasts, dragons of glass. They circled, sharp and deadly.

"Then let me see if you are worthy of what you carry."

Kaelen raised his flame instinctively. "We've endured enough trials."

The hermit's voice was cold. "Then endure one more."

The sand-beasts struck.

Lysera summoned roots from beneath the dunes, forcing life from dead earth, vines wrapping glass-dragons until they shattered. Darek darted between razor-edged storms, his daggers breaking constructs apart with speed and precision. Kaelen's flame flared, burning through the illusions until the desert itself glowed.

At last, Kaelen shouted, "Enough! We're not your enemies!"

The flame burst outward in a wave of pure defiance, scattering the glass constructs into nothing.

The hermit lowered his staff. For the first time, a faint smile creased his scarred face.

"Good. You endure. You strike not for glory, but to protect. Then perhaps... I am not too late to be of use."

The Hermit Joins

He drew closer, the sands calming around him. "I am **Kaelorin**, last of the Starward Order. I tended fragments of knowledge the Lorekeeper could not keep, though my sight is gone. I can no longer see the stars, but I remember their songs. And I would see balance restored before my bones rest here."

Kaelen's flame burned steady, as though answering the fox's whisper. Lysera bowed her head with respect, while Darek gave a low chuckle.

"Another ally. Good. Maybe with you around, we won't all die the moment the dragons find us."

Kaelorin's smile was thin, but resolute. "Then let us walk together. The Red Dragon's hunger burns closer than you think. But with knowledge, and will, even fire can be turned against itself."

Far above, on the crimson horizon, smoke began to rise.
The Red Dragon was coming.

Chapter Thirty

Songs of the Stars

Through Song, the Cosmos Remembers

The campfire burned low, its smoke carried away by the restless winds of the Glass Dunes. Around it, Kaelen, Lysera, and Darek sat weary but watchful, their newest companion silent as he traced patterns into the sand with his crystal staff.

At last, Kaelorin spoke. His voice was calm, yet carried the cadence of an old ritual, as if he were not speaking to them alone, but to the stars themselves.

"You know the Stone as a weapon, a thing the Order covets. But before it was weapon, it was song. The Eclipsera was never meant to fight—it was meant to bind."

The Stone as Song

He lifted his head, though his eyes were bound. "Every world sings, child. The rhythm of its rivers, the turning of its moons, the breath of its people—all weave into a great harmony. The Stone was forged not to command, but to *listen*. To draw those songs together into balance. That is why, when it shattered, the multiverse itself began to scream."

Lysera leaned forward, her staff glowing faintly in answer. "So each shard... still carries part of that song?"

Kaelorin nodded. "Yes. But corrupted. The Red Dragon's shard hums with hunger, the Black with fear. They twist the harmony into dissonance. To carry one is to risk hearing only their note."

Kaelen tightened his grip on the shard he bore. It pulsed faintly, like a heartbeat. "And yet the fox's flame protects me."

Kaelorin smiled faintly. "Because she remembers the true song. And she lends you her voice."

The Map of Stars

With a slow gesture, he traced his staff across the sand. Light spilled from its tip, forming constellations overhead, shimmering even against the cloud-choked sky.

"The stars are keepers of the Stone's memory. Before Kalvasar fell, my Order charted their patterns, learning how they bent toward the Stone's resonance. Look closely—"

He shifted the constellations. Three great stars flared bright: one crimson, one shadow-black, one golden. Each seemed tethered to unseen chains.

"The dragons wear their shards as crowns. But their power waxes and wanes with the stars above. The Red Dragon is strongest beneath the Blood Conjunction, when fire-stars cross the sky. Yet when the heavens fall into silence, his hunger outpaces his strength."

Darek raised a brow, his tone half-cynical, half-intrigued. "So we're meant to fight him when the sky's quiet, while he's starving?"

"Exactly," Kaelorin said simply.

The Warning

But then his tone darkened. "Do not mistake knowledge for safety. The Stone may grant you a path, but it does not walk it for you. Dragons do not fall easily. They will burn worlds before they admit weakness."

His blind gaze turned toward Kaelen, piercing despite the cloth that bound it. "You carry her flame, boy. That makes you a beacon, and a target. Avarith will not allow you to walk unchallenged."

Kaelen swallowed, the weight of his words heavy. "Then we'll have to be ready."

Kaelorin's faint smile returned, edged with steel. "Good. Because the desert burns with his hunger already. The Red Dragon comes."

And on the horizon, flames flickered against the night.

Chapter Thirty-One

Fire on the Glass Dunes

Where Light Turns to Ash

T he horizon bled red.

Winds screamed as heat surged across the Glass Dunes. The sand itself shimmered, warping into rivers of molten light. At the crest of the tallest dune, he appeared—armor crimson and burning, axe glowing white-hot, his silhouette vast against the flame.

The **Red Dragon** had come.

His voice rumbled across the desert, each word a furnace.

"You carry her light. You steal what is mine. Now I will consume you, body and soul."

Kaelen's flame burned in his palm, smaller but steady, defiance against the inferno. His breath caught, but Serenya's whisper cut through his fear:

"Do not fight fire with fire. Outlast him."

The First Clash

The Red Dragon struck first. His axe cleaved downward, a wave of molten fire ripping the dune apart. Glass shattered into the air like knives. Kaelen dove aside, the heat searing his skin even through the flame.

Lysera raised her staff, vines erupting from the sands, glowing green with desperate life. They wrapped his legs, holding him for a heartbeat—long enough for Darek to hurl his daggers into the cracks of his armor. Sparks flared, but the Red Dragon only roared, flames devouring the roots and melting steel to slag.

Kaelen's flame surged, striking the general square in the chest. For an instant, the fire recoiled. But then it blazed back, stronger, hungrier, feeding on the desert around them.

Hunger Made Flesh

The dunes screamed as they burned. The Red Dragon's flames consumed the very glass beneath his feet, twisting it into rivers of molten obsidian. His power grew with each heartbeat.

Kaelorin shouted above the roar, his staff glowing faintly with starlight. "He feeds on the land itself! We must drive him where it cannot sustain him!"

But they were surrounded by endless dunes—his feast.

Kaelen's mind raced. *The Lorekeeper said he weakens when starved. But how do we starve fire in a desert of fuel?*

Turning the Desert

Lysera's runes flared brighter than ever before, her face pale with exhaustion. "Then we deny him his feast!" She slammed her staff into the glass, pouring every ounce of her will into it.

From the scorched dunes burst roots, wide and tangled, tearing molten glass aside. They spread like a net, draining the desert of life, forcing the ground into barrenness. The Red Dragon roared as his fire found less and less to consume, the land beneath him turning brittle, gray, and dead.

Kaelen's flame seized the moment. It burned brighter, not as hunger but as defiance. He thrust it toward the general. The strike landed, cracking the crimson armor, leaving a glowing scar across his chest.

The Red Dragon staggered.

For the first time.

Retreat of Fire

His eyes burned with rage. "This is not defeat. You cannot starve me forever. The next time I burn, the worlds themselves will feed me!"

He swung his axe in fury, a final shockwave of flame that split the dune. When the fire cleared, he was gone—vanished into the storm of smoke and ash that bled across the horizon.

Aftermath

The companions stood among the wreckage, gasping. Lysera fell to her knees, her staff dim. Darek pulled her upright with gritted teeth, his hands blistered. Kaelorin leaned on his staff, his blind eyes turned to the sky.

Kaelen stared at the glowing scar his flame had carved into the Red Dragon's chest. His fist trembled, but his voice was steady.

"We can hurt them. Even generals. They're not invincible."

Lysera, pale but smiling faintly, whispered, "Endurance... is victory."

Serenya's whisper reached them, proud and fierce:

"You have proven it. Fire can falter. And shadow can bleed."

Chapter Thirty-Two

The Scar That Shouldn't Be

A Tear That Balance Cannot Heal

The chamber of the Draconis trembled.

The shards of the Eclipsera Stone pulsed unevenly, echoing the wound burned into the Red Dragon's armor. He knelt before Avarith's throne, one gauntleted hand pressed to his chest where the scar still smoldered — a crack of blue fire etched across crimson steel.

It had not healed.

The other generals stared in silence.

Mockery and Fury

The Silver Dragon broke it first, his voice sharp and cold. "A scar. From prey. Imagine it! The hunter of stars, bearer of the Forge-Axe, marked like a wounded beast by a boy's flame."

The Red Dragon's roar shook the chamber, fire searing the air. "He starved me! The dunes held no feast for flame. Were it not for barren land, he would be ash!"

The Black Dragon's voice slithered from the shadows. "And yet he is not. He endures. While you bleed."

The Red Dragon surged forward, axe raised — but Avarith's hand lifted, and the weapon froze in midair.

Avarith's Judgment

The Dark Lord rose, his obsidian armor glowing faintly with veins of molten fire. His helm tilted toward the Red Dragon, ember eyes burning.

"You bring me shame," he said simply.

The Red Dragon bowed his head, his roar breaking into silence.

But Avarith turned his gaze not on him, but on all the generals. "Do you see? Fire is not endless. Shadow is not absolute. Hunger, fear, illusion, pride—each of you carries not only power, but flaw. And now they learn them."

The Azure Dragon shifted uneasily. "If they uncover all of our weaknesses..."

"Then the Order will fracture," the Black Dragon finished, his tone almost satisfied.

The Cracks in Unity

For the first time, discord simmered openly.

The Gold Dragon's voice rumbled, heavy as stone. "Then strike now. End them. Do not let them gather more."

But the Silver Dragon smirked beneath his helm. "And risk more scars? Better to let the Red stew in his shame, while the rest of us wait for the prey to stumble. They will choke on their own courage."

The Red Dragon growled, flames rippling. "When next I face them, there will be no desert to starve me. I will burn them with the breath of a hundred worlds."

Avarith's Command

Avarith's voice cut through their bickering like a blade. "Enough."

He returned to his throne, the shards of the Stone swirling in his grasp. "You may bleed, you may fracture, but the Order is mine. They cannot yet touch me. And when the boy brings all shards together, when he walks blind into my hands, we will end both him and the fox."

He leaned forward, ember eyes narrowing.

"But until that day, bleed if you must. Let him taste small victories. Each scar will make the final breaking sweeter."

The generals bowed — some with obedience, others with doubt.

The Red Dragon's hand lingered over the scar burning his chest, his silence louder than any roar.

Chapter Thirty-Three

The Fox's Hope

A Whisper Stronger Than Chains

The crystal pulsed faintly, a heartbeat in the void.

Serenya's fox-shape curled within, her tails wrapped tight, her eyes closed against the endless dark. But tonight the chains felt lighter, not because they had broken, but because something beyond them had *shifted*.

Through the fractured echoes of the Eclipsera shards, she felt it. Rage. Discord. The Red Dragon's wound burned not only his flesh but his pride, and in the halls of the Obsidian Spire, whispers of doubt had spread like cracks through ice.

Her eyes opened, glowing blue in the crystal gloom.

"They bleed," she whispered to herself. "They fracture."

The shadows hissed in protest, trying to drown her voice. But her flame burned brighter than before.

Sensing the Generals' Discord

She reached outward through the dream-currents, brushing against the echoes of the generals.

The Red Dragon's roar, raw with fury and shame.
The Black Dragon's venomous whisper, satisfied that fear was spreading.
The Silver Dragon's arrogance, masking unease.
The Azure Dragon's doubt, a ripple beneath calm words.
Even the Gold Dragon, heavy and unmoved, felt the weight of Avarith's command pressing harder than before.

Avarith himself... still unshaken. But she felt his gaze narrow, his patience thinning.

For the first time in centuries, the Order was not iron. It was glass.

Hope Rekindled

Serenya pressed her spectral paws against the prison's walls. They still held, but the cracks of light within glowed brighter than before, pulsing with Kaelen's flame.

She whispered into the void, her voice threading through the dream-currents toward her chosen.

"You have scarred them. You have endured what none believed possible. And because of you, the dragons are no longer unbroken. This is the beginning."

The crystal shuddered faintly, not with despair but with defiance.

For the first time since her fall, Serenya dared to hope.

Chapter Thirty-Four

Ashes of the Dunes

From Flame to Dust, All Things Fade

The storm of fire had passed.

The dunes still smoked, scarred black where the Red Dragon's hunger had burned deepest. Shards of glass crunched beneath their boots as the four companions staggered into the shadow of a half-buried ruin. There, sheltered from the worst of the winds, they collapsed into the silence of survival.

Kaelen fell to his knees, his palm still glowing faintly blue. The shard pulsed weakly within his grip, but for once, its hunger felt subdued. He stared at it, the image of the Red Dragon's scar burning in his memory.

Lysera sank beside him, sweat streaking her ash-stained face. Her hands trembled as she steadied her staff, its runes dimmed from exhaustion. Yet her eyes held a faint, fierce light. "We stood against him. And he fled. We did what no one thought possible."

Darek leaned against a slab of stone, tearing a strip of cloth to wrap the blisters on his arms. He gave a sharp laugh, half-pain, half-pride. "I'd call it madness, not victory. But if scars are what we can give dragons, then maybe this fool's journey has teeth after all."

Kaelorin remained standing, his staff planted firmly in the glass, his blind gaze turned skyward. "It was not madness. It was knowledge, and will. You starved him. And for the first time, a general has learned fear."

Weighing the Victory

Kaelen raised his eyes, uncertainty flickering beneath the exhaustion. "But we didn't kill him. He'll return. Stronger."

Kaelorin's expression was grim, yet calm. "Yes. But a wound, once given, never leaves. The scar you burned into his armor is more than mark—it is reminder. Dragons believe themselves eternal, unbreakable. You shattered that belief. And in that shattering lies hope."

Lysera touched Kaelen's shoulder, her voice soft. "Hope spreads. If others learn what we did here, they may rise too."

Darek smirked, though his eyes were serious. "Or it'll make the dragons burn twice as many worlds just to prove they're still untouchable."

Kaelorin tilted his head. "Perhaps both. But the choice of what the scar means is not theirs alone. It is yours."

Bonds Forged in Fire

That night, as they shared the last of their meager rations, silence settled between them—not empty, but full, the silence of those who had faced death together and survived.

Kaelen caught himself watching the others. Lysera, leaning on her staff, her determination unbroken despite her exhaustion. Darek, sharpening his ruined daggers with stubborn care, hiding his pride beneath mockery. Kaelorin, blind yet seeing further than any of them, murmuring half-forgotten star-songs under his breath.

They were not just strangers thrown together by fate anymore. They were *companions*.

And for the first time since the fox's whisper had touched his dreams, Kaelen dared to believe they could be more than sparks in the dark.

The Road Ahead

When dawn broke, pale and gray across the wasteland, Kaelorin spoke first. "The Red Dragon will not be the last you face. Others will come. Shadows, illusions, pride, hunger—they will test you in ways fire never could."

Kaelen rose, gripping the shard tighter. "Then we'll be ready. One scar at a time, we'll prove they're not invincible."

The flame in his palm pulsed steady, its light cutting through the ash.

And far away, unseen, the Black Dragon's shadow lingered at the edge of the horizon, watching, waiting.

Chapter Thirty-Five

Roads Beyond the Ash

Through Cinders, New Paths Awaken

T he Glass Dunes lay smoldering behind them, dunes shattered by fire and scarred by roots that still clung stubbornly to the barren ground. For a day and a night they traveled in silence, each carrying the weight of what they had seen: a dragon scarred, a legend proven vulnerable.

But survival was not victory, and they all knew the Red Dragon would return.

Toward New Lands

Kaelorin led them northward, his crystal staff tapping lightly as he walked. Though blind, he moved with certainty, as if he followed paths no mortal eye could see.

"Beyond these wastes lies the **Shattered Steppe**," he said one evening as they rested against a jagged ridge. "Once a kingdom of proud riders, now broken beneath the Order's heel. Yet rumors drift of a survivor—one who defies the generals with swiftness instead of flame."

Lysera's eyes lit faintly. "Another ally?"

"Perhaps," Kaelorin replied. "The fox's song grows louder. It would not surprise me if her whispers touch others still."

Darek gave a dry chuckle. "Another outlaw to add to this little band. At this rate we'll have a whole army of misfits before long."

Kaelen, quiet until then, finally spoke. "Then we'll need them. All of them. Because if we're to face the rest of the Order, four souls won't be enough."

Trials on the Road

The journey was not easy. The Steppe had fractured long ago into broken plains and jagged chasms, shaped by battles between generals. Storms of black hail battered them, and strange beasts twisted by corruption prowled the wastes, forcing the companions to fight even when exhausted.

Yet with each trial, their unity deepened. Kaelen's flame burned steadier, now tempered by knowledge. Lysera's healing touch saved them again and again, though she grew thinner with each spell. Darek's wit cut through their fatigue as surely as his blades cut through foes. And Kaelorin's quiet wisdom gave them focus, his star-songs lifting their hearts in moments of despair.

A Glimpse of the Future

One night, they reached a cliff overlooking the fractured Steppe. Far below, faint fires dotted the plains—some the camps of Draconis patrols, but others... smaller, hidden.

"Resistance," Kaelorin murmured. "The ember still burns."

Kaelen clenched his fist, flame flickering bright in answer. "Then we'll find them. And we'll make sure it spreads."

Serenya's whisper stirred in his chest, soft but fierce:

"Yes. Sparks become flame. And flame becomes dawn."

The road stretched onward, broken but not barren. And though shadows gathered above, hope began to move across the land again.

Chapter Thirty-Six

Weavers of Lies

Threads of Deceit, Woven in Silence

The chamber of the Draconis glowed faintly with the shards of the Eclipsera Stone, pulsing like fractured hearts. The Red Dragon still bore his scar, his silence heavy with rage. The others watched him, some with contempt, others with unease.

Into that silence, the **Azure Dragon** rose.

His armor shimmered like liquid crystal, colors shifting with each movement. Where the Red was brute flame and the Black was shadow made flesh, the Azure was deception incarnate. His helm bore no mouth, no eyes—only a mirrored surface that reflected whatever looked upon it.

"My brothers and sisters," his voice slid across the chamber, smooth as silk. "We send fire, we send shadow, and yet the fox's sparks still endure. Perhaps it is time we remind them: not all battles are fought in the body."

The Nature of Azure

He lifted one gauntleted hand, and from it spilled a haze of light. The generals watched as the haze twisted into shapes—Kaelen, Lysera, Darek, and even the blind hermit Kaelorin. Their forms were perfect, yet subtly wrong: Kaelen's flame burned black, Lysera's vines strangled, Darek's blades dripped blood, and Kaelorin's staff cracked into shards.

"The mind," the Azure whispered, "is more fragile than flesh. Break what they believe, and they will tear themselves apart without a blade raised against them."

The Silver Dragon laughed lightly, cruel and amused. "And how do you propose to shatter their minds, Weaver?"

The Azure tilted his mirrored helm. "By showing them the futures they most fear. By twisting their bonds until they no longer know who they are. Hope burns bright—but hope can be poisoned."

Discord Among the Order

The Black Dragon stirred, shadows curling at his feet. "Deception is a coward's tool. Shadows alone could silence them forever."

The Red Dragon growled, flames hissing from his cracked armor. "Enough of tricks. Give me land to burn, and I will end them."

But Avarith raised his hand, and silence fell.

His ember gaze fixed on the Azure Dragon. "Fire failed. Shadow faltered. Perhaps it is time to weave illusion into the tapestry of their path. Let them see what they cannot endure—let them doubt themselves until their flame gutters out."

The Azure bowed, his shimmering form bending like water. "It will be done, my lord."

The Loom of Illusions

When the generals departed, the Azure Dragon remained behind, alone in the chamber. He spread his hands, and light poured across the shards of the Stone.

Within that light, visions formed.

Kaelen stood over his companions, flame gone black.
Lysera fell with her staff broken, her vines strangling Kaelen's throat.
Darek raised his blades, not against enemies, but against his allies.
And Serenya—the fox—watched, silent, her crystal prison cracked into a thousand mirrors.

The Azure's voice was soft, almost tender.
"Let them see their end. And let them believe it is truth."

The illusions dissolved into mist, carried into the dream-currents.

The hunt of flame and shadow had failed.
Now the war of the mind would begin.

Chapter Thirty-Seven

Shadows in the Mind

Whispers That Fracture the Soul

T he road beyond the Glass Dunes was quiet at first, too quiet. The winds softened, the skies cleared, and for a time, the companions almost felt as though the worst had passed.

But the illusions came not with thunder or flame — they came in silence.

Kaelen's Doubt

It began with Kaelen.

One evening, as the group made camp among broken stones, he swore he saw Serenya's fox-shape standing just beyond the firelight. She looked at him, eyes glowing, her voice soft:

"You cannot save them. Every scar you give the dragons will cost you more. They will fall, one by one, because of you."

He stumbled forward, reaching out. But when he touched her, she dissolved into ash, and in her place lay Lysera's broken staff.

The flame in his palm flared violently, and when he blinked—his companions were staring at him in alarm.

"Kaelen?" Lysera asked, her tone sharp. "What did you see?"

"...Nothing," he lied, but his voice shook.

Lysera's Vision

The next night, it was Lysera. She dreamed of her healing roots spreading across the wasteland, bringing green life back to the barren earth. But then the vines blackened, tightening around Kaelen's throat. His flame sputtered, his eyes turned hollow, and with a final gasp, he whispered: *"You killed me."*

She awoke screaming, her staff glowing uncontrollably. It took Kaelorin's calm hand on her shoulder and a murmured star-song to steady her again.

"They are illusions," he said firmly. "Not truth. Remember that."

But Lysera could not shake the image of Kaelen's lifeless face.

Darek's Betrayal

On the third night, Darek vanished.

Kaelen and Lysera found him at dawn, crouched by the ridge with both daggers drawn, his breath ragged. When they approached, he turned on them, blades flashing.

"You think I'll betray you, don't you?" he snapped, eyes wild. "I saw it. I saw myself driving steel into your backs. And you let it happen. You *knew*."

Kaelen stepped back, flame ready, heart pounding. But Lysera stood between them, her voice steady. "Darek. That wasn't you. That was what they wanted you to see."

For a long, tense moment, Darek's blades trembled in his grip. Then he dropped them, sinking to his knees. "If they can make me see it... what's to stop me from doing it?"

Kaelorin's blind eyes turned toward him. "Because you choose otherwise. That is the difference between illusion and truth."

The Unseen War

By the fourth day, none of them trusted what they saw. Shapes shifted on the horizon. Whispers followed them in the wind. Sometimes, they even doubted each other—Kaelen swore Lysera's eyes glowed with corruption, Lysera thought she heard Darek muttering to shadows, Darek claimed Kaelorin's lantern-light led them in circles.

But each time, Kaelorin's calm voice anchored them:

"Hold fast. Illusion cannot kill you. Only your belief in it can."

Still, Kaelen could feel the Azure Dragon's presence, subtle but suffocating. The illusions were not random—they were tailored to each of them, cutting at their deepest fears.

And in the distance, the shimmer of the Shattered Steppe loomed, hazy and uncertain.

Were they walking toward an ally... or another illusion?

Chapter Thirty-Eight

The Trial of False Dawn

Where Shadows Wear the Mask of Morning

The night fell heavy on the wasteland. No stars broke through the clouds. No winds stirred the dunes.

And then—silence fractured.

A shimmer of blue light passed over the camp, subtle and cold. Kaelen felt his flame gutter, then flare too bright. When he blinked, the world around him had changed.

Kaelen's Nightmare

He stood alone in a burning village. His village. The sky above cracked with dragonfire. His father's voice called for him, but when Kaelen ran, the voice twisted into a scream.

From the flames stepped Serenya—not the fox, but the princess in her true form, armor radiant. She looked at him with sorrow in her eyes.

"You will fail as I did," she said, her blade dripping with ash. "And because of you, the worlds will burn."

The shard in Kaelen's hand pulsed, whispering: *"Unless you embrace me. Take my hunger. Become fire."*

His flame faltered. His choice trembled before him.

Lysera's Nightmare

Lysera wandered through an endless field of vines, green and thriving. At first it filled her with peace—until the vines coiled tighter, their flowers dripping blood. They wrapped around her arms, her throat, her staff.

She tried to heal them, but her magic only deepened their corruption.

Kaelen appeared in the distance, gasping, choking in the vines. Darek followed, dragged down into roots that bound his limbs. Kaelorin stood further still, silent, his blind eyes turned away.

The vines whispered: *"Your gift is poison. Everything you touch dies."*

Her staff cracked in her hands.

Darek's Nightmare

Darek ran through alleys he knew too well. The city of his youth, filled with shadows of people he had once betrayed. Friends. Lovers. Companions long dead.

Every corner he turned, their voices followed: *"You left us. You sold us. You ran."*

And at the end of the alley, Kaelen and Lysera stood, eyes full of the same accusation.

"You'll do it again," Kaelen said, voice cold.

"You'll leave us to die," Lysera whispered.

Darek's daggers turned red in his hands, dripping blood he couldn't wash away.

Kaelorin's Nightmare

The hermit stood in darkness. Above him, the stars were gone. Silent. Dead. He stretched out his hands, but no constellations sang, no Stone pulsed with harmony.

"Blind," a voice hissed. "You have always been blind. Your wisdom is ash. Your hope is silence."

And in that silence, he felt himself vanish—irrelevant, forgotten, dust.

The Breaking Point

Each of them fought alone. Each trapped in their private ruin. The Azure Dragon's voice whispered through every vision:

"Hope is fragile. Break it, and they will shatter themselves."

And in the real world, their bodies twisted in restless sleep, caught in the nightmare. The Azure Dragon's illusion had bound them all.

Only Kaelen's flame flickered faintly against the illusion, a thread of light refusing to die. Serenya's whisper echoed faintly into his dream, soft and urgent:

"This is not truth. Remember—endurance is choice. Choose the flame."

Chapter Thirty-Nine

The Flame of Defiance

Born of Ash, It Burns Unbroken

K aelen knelt in the burning ruins of his village, Serenya's spectral form standing before him with her blade dripping ash, her words ringing like a verdict:

"You will fail as I did. The worlds will burn because of you."

The shard pulsed in his hand, whispering louder: *"Take me. Feed me. Only fire can stand against fire. Let me burn for you."*

Kaelen's knees buckled. His father's scream tore the air. His mother's face, burning, reached for him through the flames. Everything in him wanted to give in—to wield the shard's hunger, to silence the voices of failure with destruction.

And then—another whisper. Softer, but fierce.

"This is not truth. It is the shadow of fear. Choose the flame, Kaelen. Not fire's hunger, but defiance."

Serenya.

Kaelen shut his eyes, clutching the shard and flame together. His voice trembled, but he forced the words through his teeth:

"No. I am not your weapon. I am not your failure. I am Kaelen—and I endure."

The blue flame in his hand burst outward, burning away the black fire, silencing the screams. Serenya's figure flickered—not as the accusing warrior, but as the fox again, her eyes warm.

"Yes. That is the truth. Now free them."

Breaking the Illusions

The flame spread, tearing through the false village. Kaelen gasped awake, the real wasteland night pressing around him. His companions writhed in their sleep, caught in their own nightmares. Lysera's staff glowed dangerously, Darek's daggers shook in his hands, Kaelorin's lips moved in wordless despair.

The flame in Kaelen's palm wavered, but he pushed it toward them, touching each with its light.

Lysera's Freedom

He placed the flame to Lysera's staff. In her nightmare, the vines choking Kaelen and Darek burst into flowers. Her tears turned to light, and she realized: *"My gift heals, not destroys."* She awoke, gasping, clutching Kaelen's hand.

Darek's Freedom

He touched the flame to Darek's daggers. In the alley of ghosts, the accusations dissolved. Kaelen and Lysera looked at him not with scorn, but with trust. Darek spat into the dark, snarling: *"I decide who I stand with. And I don't run this time."* He awoke, panting, but his grip on his blades was steady.

Kaelorin's Freedom

Last, he pressed the flame to Kaelorin's staff. In the void of silent stars, one light flared. Then another. Until the constellations blazed once more. Kaelorin smiled faintly, whispering: *"Blind, yes. But never lost."* He awoke, calm, his hands folded over his staff.

Together Again

The four sat in the pale firelight, breaths heavy, sweat clinging to them. None spoke for a long while.

Finally, Darek broke the silence. "That wasn't just a dream. That was him. The Azure."

Lysera shivered. "He tried to turn us against ourselves. To make us doubt who we are."

Kaelen's flame flickered steady in his palm. "And he nearly did. But we endured. Together."

Kaelorin inclined his head, his blind eyes solemn. "Illusion is the deadliest weapon, for it does not strike the body, but the will. Tonight, you proved yours still holds."

Serenya's whisper reached them, faint but fierce:

"Yes. You endure. And while you endure, hope cannot be broken."

Chapter Forty

The Weaver's Fracture

A Tear Woven Into Destiny

T he Azure Dragon knelt before the shards of the Eclipsera, his mirrored helm rippling like water disturbed. The reflections within it showed not his own form, but the four companions — Kaelen's flame steady, Lysera's staff unbroken, Darek's daggers gleaming, Kaelorin's lantern glowing with calm defiance.

They had endured.

His voice, usually smooth and liquid, cracked with venom. "They resisted me. They *resisted me.* My illusions are flawless. They should have drowned in their own fear."

Fury in the Spire

The Red Dragon's laughter rumbled through the chamber, bitter and cruel. "So the master of lies is unmasked. Your phantoms shattered by a boy's flame. Perhaps you are weaker than you claim."

The Azure Dragon's form shimmered with anger, the mirrors on his armor twisting to reflect the Red's wound — the scar of blue fire across crimson steel. "And you would mock me? At least I did not fall to *hunger*."

The Red surged to his feet, fire boiling in his helm. "Say it again, and I will burn your illusions into ash!"

"Enough," Avarith's voice thundered, silencing them both.

Avarith's Warning

The Dark Lord's ember gaze fixed on the Azure Dragon. "Do not let fury consume you. Your illusions failed because you underestimated them. Not because they are flawless, but because their bond is stronger than you believed."

The Azure bowed, his shimmering form dim. "Then they will pay for it. I will unravel that bond thread by thread until nothing remains but ashes of trust."

Avarith leaned forward, his voice iron and fire. "See that you do. They cannot be allowed to carry their hope into the Steppe. Break them before they find more allies, or you will answer to me."

The shards of the Stone pulsed like a heartbeat, the chamber vibrating with their fractured song.

The Azure Dragon rose, his mirrored helm reflecting nothing but blackness. "Then let them dream of strength. I will make their unity their undoing."

And with that, he dissolved into shimmering mist, vanishing into the dream-currents once more.

Chapter Forty-One

The Fox's Vigil

Through Silence, the Watch Endures

W ithin her crystal prison, Serenya shuddered.

The dream-currents rippled like a stormed sea, carrying with them the fury of the Azure Dragon. His illusions had been broken. His perfect web of lies torn apart by Kaelen's flame, Lysera's will, Darek's stubbornness, and Kaelorin's calm.

She felt his rage bleed outward — a scream without sound, a mirror shattering across the infinite dark.

But instead of despair, Serenya smiled.

Hope Through the Storm

She pressed her paws against the crystal walls, her blue light glowing brighter. "Yes, Azure. Rage. Rage, because they are stronger than your lies. Rage, because you cannot unmake the bond they forge."

The shadows hissed around her, trying to smother her defiance. But every hiss only reminded her of the Order's fear.

"They bleed," she whispered to the silence. "They fracture. And still, my sparks endure."

Reaching to Kaelen

She let her light spread through the dream-currents, threading toward Kaelen and the others. She could not free herself yet, but she could reach them.

Her voice touched Kaelen's dreams like a flame in the dark.

"You did not break. You chose truth. That is your strength — and mine. They will come again, hungrier, more desperate. But remember this: every failure of theirs weakens my prison. Every victory of yours cracks their dominion."

The crystal pulsed faintly, tiny fissures spreading like veins of light. Not enough to shatter — not yet. But enough to remind her: the tide was turning.

The Vigil

Serenya curled her tails around herself, her sapphire eyes burning.

"I will endure, as you endure. And when the chains finally break, I will stand beside you once more."

The shadows hissed louder, but the fox's hope rang stronger.

The Azure Dragon had failed. And Serenya knew now — the generals could be defeated, not only in flesh, but in spirit.

Chapter Forty-Two

Riders of the Shattered Steppe

Hooves Across a Broken Horizon

The wastelands gave way to broken plains. Great cracks split the earth, some wide as rivers, others shallow but endless, scars left from battles where dragon and mortal once clashed. Sparse grasses clung to life among the fractures, waving in winds that carried both dust and the faint scent of smoke.

This was the **Shattered Steppe**.

First Impressions

Kaelen paused at the ridge, his flame flickering against the twilight. "It feels different here," he murmured. "Not dead like the dunes. Not alive either. Just... wounded."

Kaelorin's blind eyes tilted toward the horizon. "The Steppe once sang of freedom. Its riders were swift as stormwinds, their banners bright against the sky. But the Order broke them. What you smell now is the ash of villages burned to silence."

Lysera's staff hummed softly as she pressed it into the ground. "And yet—something endures. I can feel it in the soil. A heartbeat. Faint, but alive."

Darek smirked faintly, though his eyes scanned the plains with wariness. "Alive usually means dangerous. Which means we're walking straight into trouble."

The First Sign

As night settled, the companions made camp near a fractured hill. The winds grew restless, carrying whispers too steady to be accident. Hooves thundered faintly in the distance, then faded before they could rise to pursuit.

Kaelen stood sharply, flame burning brighter. "You hear that?"

Darek's hand went to his daggers. "Riders. Watching."

But when Kaelen looked to the horizon, he saw only shadows moving against starlight—too swift, too distant to be certain if they were real or illusion.

Kaelorin's voice was calm. "If the rider you seek yet lives, he will test you before he reveals himself. The Steppe bows to none but strength and spirit."

A Flicker of Challenge

At dawn, they found the first sign of deliberate contact.

Carved into the stone at the edge of their camp was a symbol—a horse's head etched in swift lines, its eyes burning with defiance. Beneath it lay a shard of glass arrowhead, sharpened and new.

A message, left for them.

Lysera touched the symbol with reverence. "The riders still live."

Darek scowled, but there was awe in his voice. "Or at least one does. And he knows we're here."

Kaelen clenched his fist around the shard he bore. "Then we'll prove we're worth finding. We need allies—and if the Steppe still rides, maybe we'll find them here."

Far away, the echo of hooves thundered again, closer this time. The fox's whisper stirred in Kaelen's chest, fierce and hopeful:

"Yes. Seek him. For not all flames are bound to dragons."

The hunt for the Steppe rider had begun.

Chapter Forty-Three

Whispers of Hooves

Echoes Carried on the Steppe Wind

The Steppe stretched vast before them, broken by ridges and chasms, its silence pierced only by the hiss of wind. Yet the companions knew they were not alone.

Every night, the thunder of hooves echoed in the distance. Never close enough to see, but near enough to remind them that eyes were always watching.

The First Trial — The Arrow

On the second morning, they found another sign.

An arrow, black-fletched, pierced their waterskin where it hung by the fire. The shaft quivered faintly, still warm from flight. Not a warning, not a kill — but a test.

Darek yanked it free, scowling. "Could've taken my head if he wanted to. He's playing with us."

Kaelorin's blind eyes turned toward the plains. "Not play. Judgment. He measures who you are, not what you carry."

Lysera touched the arrowhead. "He wants to know if we'll endure thirst as we endured fire."

The Second Trial — The Herd

That evening, they crossed a ridge and saw them — wild horses running across the Steppe, swift as wind, manes like banners. Their beauty was almost painful, a glimpse of what the land had been before dragonfire.

But as the herd thundered past, Kaelen noticed one shape among them that was wrong: a rider cloaked in black, moving in perfect rhythm with the horses, his face hidden. When Kaelen blinked, he was gone, as if the Steppe itself had swallowed him.

"Did you see—" Kaelen began.

Lysera nodded, pale. "Yes."

The Third Trial — The Fire Ring

On the third night, the trial turned deadly.

They woke to find their camp surrounded by a ring of fire, arrows burning where they had struck the sand. The flames drew closer, a slow circle of heat.

Kaelen raised his flame, but Kaelorin lifted a hand. "No. This is not meant to kill. It is meant to see how you respond."

Darek cursed, blades flashing. "Then let's show him."

Together, they broke through the weakest side of the fire, Kaelen's flame parting the blaze, Lysera's staff shielding them, Darek cutting a path, and Kaelorin guiding them by instinct. They emerged coughing, burned but alive.

And when the smoke cleared, another symbol was etched in the sand beyond the ashes — a horse's head, flanked by wings.

A promise. Or a challenge.

The Rider's Shadow

By dawn, they knew.

The Steppe rider was real. He had tested them — thirst, fear, fire. And still he had not shown his face.

Kaelen clenched his fist, his flame burning steady. "Then we'll keep walking until he does. We've endured dragons. We'll endure him too."

The fox's whisper stirred faintly in his chest:

"Good. For he is more than ally. He is storm. And storms choose only the strong."

Chapter Forty-Four

The Storm Rider

Where Lightning Finds Its Master

The fourth night on the Steppe, the ambush came.

The companions had made camp in a shallow ravine, sheltered from the wind. The fire burned low, their bodies heavy with exhaustion. For a time, it seemed the plains would give them peace.

But then came the thunder.

Hooves roared across the Steppe, echoing from every side. Shadows swept along the ridges, circling the ravine. Before Kaelen could rise, arrows hissed from the darkness, striking the ground near their fire, a circle of steel hemming them in.

Then—silence.

From the ridge above, a single rider appeared. Cloaked in black, his horse tall and wild-eyed, mane whipping in the wind. His bow gleamed in the starlight, arrow drawn and aimed straight at Kaelen's heart.

The Rider's Challenge

"You've trespassed on the Steppe," the rider's voice rang, sharp as the wind. "And you carry fire. Speak your purpose, or die where you kneel."

Kaelen rose slowly, flame flickering in his palm. "We came seeking you. The one who still rides free beneath the dragons' shadow. We need allies."

The rider's arrow did not waver. "Allies are forged in blood. Prove you are not the Order's pawns. Prove you are not prey."

With a cry, he loosed the arrow.

Kaelen barely deflected it with his flame before the rider spurred his horse down the ridge, charging into the ravine.

The Battle of the Ravine

The rider moved like storm and steel. His horse leapt the ravine's rocks with impossible speed, while his bow loosed arrow after arrow in perfect rhythm. Each shaft was a test—aimed not to kill outright, but to force them to *survive*.

Lysera's staff swept arcs of green light, deflecting arrows with roots that burst from stone. Darek darted forward, blades flashing, but the rider's spear swung down in answer, knocking him sprawling.

Kaelen's flame roared, forcing the rider back. Yet every strike of fire was answered by speed—the horse twisting away, the rider striking from new angles, relentless as the wind itself.

Proving Themselves

Finally, Kaelen planted his feet, the flame burning steady. "We're not your enemies!" he shouted, forcing the rider's next arrow to meet his flame head-on. The blue fire burned bright, splitting the arrow in midair.

Darek staggered back to his feet, daggers raised. "If we were weak, we'd be dead by now. If we were Draconis, you'd already be ash!"

Lysera's staff glowed fiercely, her voice clear. "We fight because the worlds bleed! If you stand against the Order, then so do we!"

The rider drew back, horse skidding to a halt in the dust. His bow lowered.

The Rider Revealed

Slowly, he pulled back his hood, revealing a scarred but proud face, eyes burning with defiance. His voice lost its edge, though not its strength.

"Few endure the trials of the Steppe. Fewer still stand against fire and shadow. You are sparks, yes... but perhaps sparks that may yet become a storm."

He raised his spear in salute. "I am **Ravyn, last of the Steppe Riders.** If you would stand with me, then together we may ride against dragons."

The fox's whisper stirred in Kaelen's chest, fierce with pride:

"Yes. The storm has answered."

Chapter Forty-Five

Fractures in the Spire

The Cracks That Echo Through Heaven

The shards of the Eclipsera pulsed unevenly in the Obsidian Spire, their fractured song filled with dissonance. Avarith sat silent upon his throne as the generals gathered, their gazes fixed upon the newest whisper carried by the dream-currents:

A rider still lived.

The General's Reactions

The Red Dragon's roar filled the chamber. "Lies! We burned the Steppe to glass. We *erased* its riders. None could have survived."

The Azure Dragon's mirrored helm tilted, his voice a silken hiss. "And yet whispers spread of hooves on the wind. If even one rider still breathes, then the Order's dominion is not as complete as we claim."

The Silver Dragon laughed cruelly. "How fitting. Fire leaves scars, shadow fails, illusion shatters—and now ghosts of old rebellions ride again. Tell me, brothers—shall we tremble at the sound of hooves?"

The Red surged to his feet, flames spilling. "Mock me again and I'll scorch your tongue from your helm."

Avarith's Silence

The chamber shook with their discord until Avarith finally spoke. His voice was calm, but carried weight enough to silence even the Red.

"One rider is not an army."

His ember eyes narrowed, gaze piercing through the mist of the shards. "But symbols are more dangerous than armies. The Steppe was broken to remind the worlds that no rebellion could endure. If this rider still lives, then hope survives where none should."

He rose, obsidian armor glowing faintly with molten veins. "And hope spreads faster than fire."

Orders Given

Avarith's voice hardened into command.

"Red. You will heal your scar and burn the Steppe again. Show them no field can shelter resistance."

"Azure. Weave lies among the mortals. Turn whispers of riders into tales of monsters, until none know truth from dream."

"Black. Hunt from the shadows. Drive fear into any who look to the plains for courage."

The generals bowed—some in obedience, some in simmering resentment. The Order was still bound, but the cracks in their unity widened with every failure, every spark of resistance.

The Fox's Watch

From within her crystal, Serenya felt it. The discord in the Spire. The whisper of hooves echoing against dragonfire.

Her light pulsed faintly, a smile ghosting across her fox-shape.

"Yes... let them fear. For the world remembers what they would have it forget."

Chapter Forty-Six

The Rider's Oath

The Promise Carved in Tempest

The dawn over the Steppe was painted in gold and gray. Dust hung in the air from the clash of the night before. Kaelen and the others stood still, catching their breath, while the rider known as **Ravyn** dismounted. His boots struck the stone with a weight that carried both pride and sorrow.

He looked at each of them in turn — Kaelen with his flame, Lysera clutching her staff, Darek wiping blood from a shallow cut, Kaelorin silent but steady with his staff of crystal.

"You endured," Ravyn said simply. His voice carried no apology for the trial, only recognition. "Few outsiders would have survived my tests. Fewer still would have stood together through them. The Steppe bows to no one... but perhaps, it will ride with you."

The Story of the Steppe

That evening, as the companions gathered around the fire, Ravyn shared his tale.

He spoke of the **Steppe Riders**, once the fastest army of the free worlds. They were not conquerors but guardians, their horses swift as the wind, their bows striking from beyond reach. When the Draconis came, the Riders were the first to answer.

"And the first to fall," Ravyn said, bitterness rough in his tone. "We fought the Red Dragon in open plain. Fire devoured the grasslands, and the sky rained ash. Thousands fell. By the battle's end, I alone remained."

Lysera's eyes softened. "And still you rode."

Ravyn nodded. "Because someone had to. The Steppe remembers. The hooves of one rider can still thunder louder than silence."

Trust Forged

Darek leaned back, smirking faintly. "Well, you've got a flair for the dramatic. But what I want to know is — if you've been riding free all this time, why not join others sooner?"

Ravyn's gaze cut to him, sharp as an arrow. "Because trust is not given. It is proven. Just as you had to prove yours."

Kaelen met his eyes, flame flickering steady. "Then ride with us. The dragons bleed. We've seen it. Together, we can make them bleed again."

For the first time, Ravyn's stern face cracked into a thin, dangerous smile. "Then let the Steppe ride once more."

The Fox's Whisper

That night, as the campfire burned low, Kaelen felt Serenya's whisper stir within him, proud and bright.

"Yes... gather them. Each ally is another thread in the tapestry of balance. The Order broke the Steppe, but you have made it rise again. You are no longer sparks alone. You are the beginning of a storm."

Kaelen's fist clenched, the flame steady against the night.

They were not alone anymore.

Chapter Forty-Seven

Echoes of Hooves in the Spire

When Thunder Walks the Hollow Heights

T he Obsidian Spire trembled with discord. The shards of the Eclipsera Stone glowed fitfully, their fractured song resonating with something that should not exist:

the thunder of hooves.

The Revelation

The Red Dragon snarled, flames seething from the scar still etched across his chestplate. "Impossible. The Steppe was ash! I saw them burn. None could have endured my fire!"

The Silver Dragon's laughter rang cruel and mocking. "And yet one rides. Imagine it — your inferno could not finish what you boasted was absolute. Perhaps your scar runs deeper than armor, brother."

The Red Dragon's roar shook the chamber, but his fury could not smother the truth.

The Generals Divide

The Black Dragon's voice cut through the tension, low and venomous. "Symbols are more dangerous than swords. One rider is not an army, yet the worlds will hear his hooves and remember what it is to resist."

The Azure Dragon's mirrored helm gleamed faintly, his tone cool as glass. "Then perhaps we should thank him. A symbol draws mortals into the open. And symbols are fragile things, easier to shatter before all than to smother in silence."

The Gold Dragon rumbled, slow and grave. "If he lives, it means the Order's victory was never complete. That is weakness. We cannot permit it to spread."

Avarith Speaks

From his throne, Avarith rose. His voice cut across the chamber like a blade.

"You bicker like carrion over scraps. Hear me well: the rider's survival is not the failure of one, but the danger of all. The Steppe is memory. Memory of freedom. Memory of a time before fire and shadow."

His ember gaze swept across them, molten and cold all at once. "And memory inspires rebellion."

He lifted his hand, and the shards of the Stone pulsed violently, their fractured light dancing like broken stars.

"Burn the Steppe again. Drown its whispers in fear. And when the rider shows himself — break him before the eyes of the worlds, so that none may mistake defiance for hope."

Serenya's Vigil

In her crystal, Serenya felt the ripples of their fury. She pressed her tails close, her eyes burning.

"Yes. Fear them, dragons. Fear the sound of hooves. For you thought the Steppe dead, and yet it rises. You thought sparks could not endure, and yet they burn brighter."

The cracks of hope spread wider through the dream-currents.

The storm was gathering.

Chapter Forty-Eight

Whispers of the Steppe

The Wind Speaks in Forgotten Tongues

The Shattered Steppe was not empty.

Beneath its burned plains and fractured ridges, survivors still endured — hiding in ruined villages, wandering with broken clans, or eking out life as hunters and outlaws. For years, they had lived beneath silence, believing the Riders gone forever.

But now... hooves thundered again.

The Village of Ashen Wells

In the ruins of Ashen Wells, where children fetched water from cracked cisterns, a scout burst into the square. His voice rang with awe, not fear:

"I saw him. A Rider. Black cloak, bow like starlight, horse swift as storm. He rode against strangers, tested them in fire — and lived."

At first, none believed him. But when he showed the arrow, fletched in the old Steppe style, whispers rippled through the crowd. Mothers clutched their children, elders wept silently, and the young stood taller.

"The Steppe still rides," someone breathed.

The Camp of Broken Banners

Far across the plains, outlaws camped in the shadow of burned banners. They gathered around a fire as one of their number returned from scouting.

"He lives," she said simply, laying down a carved horse's head found etched in the sand.

The men and women stared, and for the first time in years, laughter broke out — harsh, defiant, alive.

"If Ravyn rides, then so will we," one swore. "The dragons bled our families, but they will bleed in turn."

The Rising Rumor

The whispers spread like wildfire. Across the Steppe, scattered bands began to raise their old symbols — crude horse-marks etched into stone, banners sewn from scraps, songs half-remembered but sung again beneath the stars.

They were not yet an army. They were not even unified. But they had something they had not dared to claim in decades.

Hope.

Serenya's Light

In her crystal, Serenya felt the echo of those whispers — fragile, but growing. The Steppe's song, once silenced, began to stir again.

Her fox-shape glowed faintly, her eyes fierce. *"Yes. Let them remember. Let them rise. The Order cannot kill memory. And memory, when fed by hope, becomes rebellion."*

The cracks in the dark widened a little more.

The storm was no longer only four companions — it was beginning to spread.

Chapter Forty-Nine

Lessons of the Steppe

What the Wind Teaches, None Forget

The plains stretched wide beneath the dawn, the wind carrying dust and the scent of wild horses. It was here, among the cracked ridges of the Shattered Steppe, that **Ravyn** began his teaching.

The Rider's Demands

"You fought fire and shadow," Ravyn told them, spear planted in the earth. "But dragons are not your only enemy. To ride the Steppe is to fight the world itself—wind, distance, hunger, and time. If you cannot master these, you will die long before you ever face another general."

He mounted his horse in one fluid motion, his scarred face stern. "Today, you learn to endure as the Steppe endures."

Kaelen's Trial — Flame and Balance

Ravyn placed Kaelen on a spare horse, lean and restless. "Your flame is your strength, boy. But fire is useless if you cannot aim it from a moving mount."

Kaelen struggled at first—his flame sputtering as the horse surged beneath him, his strikes wild and unsteady. More than once he nearly toppled, earning Ravyn's sharp rebuke.

"Control is not fire's nature. It is *yours.*"

By day's end, Kaelen managed to steady his flame into a narrow strike, cutting a target Ravyn had hung from a broken post. For the first time, the Rider's hard expression flickered into approval.

Lysera's Trial — Roots in Motion

For Lysera, the challenge was stranger still. Ravyn ordered her to summon her vines while riding, forcing her to weave green life into the barren earth without stopping.

At first, her roots faltered, torn apart by speed and dust. But she pressed on, sweat pouring, determination unbroken. Finally, she coaxed a net of vines to rise even as her horse galloped, snaring a target Ravyn had loosed into the wind.

"You heal, you bind, you create," Ravyn said. "Even in motion. That is the Steppe's way."

Darek's Trial — Blades and Wind

Darek was given the simplest task: strike moving targets while his horse ran. Yet Ravyn drove him harder than the others, loosing clay jars into the wind at impossible angles, forcing him to push his reflexes past instinct.

When he cursed, Ravyn only smirked. "If you can strike a jar in wind, you can strike a dragon's eye."

By dusk, Darek's daggers split one jar midair, earning him a rare grin from the Rider.

Kaelorin's Trial — Stars on the Steppe

Kaelorin, blind but unshaken, was set a trial of endurance: to guide them across the Steppe by listening to the wind and sky. Ravyn doubted at first—but as they rode through a storm, it was Kaelorin who found their path, leading them unerringly to shelter.

"The stars may be hidden," he murmured, "but their song remains."

Even Ravyn bowed his head in respect.

Bonds Forged in Dust and Sweat

By nightfall, the companions collapsed in exhaustion, their bodies aching, but their spirits sharpened. Ravyn sat apart, sharpening his spear by the fire, but his eyes lingered on them with something close to pride.

"You have the bones of riders," he said at last. "Not yet the storm. But perhaps... one day."

Kaelen's flame flickered steady, and Serenya's whisper stirred within him, fierce and proud:

"Yes. Learn. Endure. For every lesson carries you closer to the dawn."

The Steppe had begun to teach them. And with it, the storm grew stronger.

Chapter Fifty

Trial of the Beast

The Monster Without, The Beast Within

D ays bled into weeks, the companions rising before dawn to ride until their muscles screamed, their hands blistered, their magic drained. Ravyn drove them mercilessly, but each night by the fire he saw the steel they were forging together.

"Endurance makes a rider," he told them. "But skill makes you storm."

Sharpened Lessons

- **Kaelen** learned to weave his flame into arcs that could strike without losing balance in the saddle, his blue fire becoming an extension of horse and rider alike.

- **Lysera** mastered the art of calling roots and vines in motion, her magic snaring targets with precision even at full gallop.

- **Darek** pushed his reflexes to the edge, striking airborne clay disks Ravyn hurled without warning, until his daggers moved like lightning.

- **Kaelorin** taught them all patience, guiding them by listening to wind and ground when vision faltered, reminding them that wisdom was as sharp as any blade.

Their bond deepened in dust, sweat, and bruises. Yet Ravyn knew drills were not enough.

The Beast in the Steppe

One evening, as the sun bled red into the plains, Ravyn led them toward a jagged gorge. His voice was grim.

"Training ends when you face death. The Steppe is not kind, and neither is the Order's corruption. Tonight, you face a true enemy."

From the gorge rose a sound like grinding stone. Then it emerged — a **corrupted beast**, once a proud stallion of the Steppe, now twisted by dragonfire. Its hide was cracked glass, its mane a blaze of ash, its eyes glowing crimson. Chains of molten shadow wrapped its limbs, dragging as it moved, yet its speed was terrifying.

Kaelen's stomach clenched. "What... is it?"

Ravyn's eyes hardened. "A rider's horse, broken in the Red Dragon's fire. To ride the Steppe, you must conquer what the Steppe lost."

The Trial Begins

The beast charged.

Kaelen's flame flared as he veered his horse aside, the corrupted stallion's hooves shattering stone where he had stood. Lysera's staff bloomed roots across the ground, but the beast tore through them, ash burning where flowers had sprouted.

Darek rode straight into its path, drawing its focus with flashing daggers. "Come on then, ugly—let's dance!"

Kaelorin raised his staff, murmuring a star-song that steadied the others' hearts even as the beast's roar shook the gorge.

Breaking the Corruption

They fought not to kill, but to *free.*

Kaelen hurled his flame in steady bursts, not enough to consume, but enough to burn away the chains. Lysera poured healing magic into the cracks in its hide, vines wrapping its legs to hold it steady. Darek slashed the chains loose one by one, his blades glowing red from the heat.

At last, Kaelen pressed his flame directly against the beast's chest. The corruption screamed, shattering in a burst of black smoke.

The stallion collapsed, panting, its eyes clearing to a faint, exhausted blue. No longer twisted.

Ravyn dismounted, kneeling by its side, his expression softened. He touched its neck, and for the first time his voice was not hard, but reverent. "The Steppe remembers."

The Storm Grows

That night, around the fire, Ravyn raised his spear to the sky. "You are no longer strangers. You are riders of the Steppe, in part if not in blood. And with you, the Steppe will ride again."

Kaelen's flame burned steady in his palm. Serenya's whisper echoed proud and fierce:

"Yes. The storm grows. And soon, even dragons will tremble at its thunder."

Chapter Fifty-One

The Shadow's Hunt

Every Step Follows in Silence

The chamber was cold. No flame, no light, only the pulse of the fractured Stone. In that silence, the **Black Dragon** stood apart from his brothers, his armor like liquid night, shifting with every breath.

Where the Red Dragon roared and the Azure wove illusions, the Black moved without sound. His power was not in open battle but in terror — the whisper before death, the shadow that swallowed hope.

Now Avarith's gaze fell upon him.

"Flame scarred. Illusion resisted. It is time fear walks again. Go to the Steppe. Do not strike to kill — yet. Break them slowly. Hunt them until their courage rots into despair."

The Black Dragon bowed his helm. "As you command."

The Nature of the Black Dragon

As he turned to leave the chamber, shadows bled from his armor, filling the air like smoke. Wherever they touched the ground, the stone itself cracked and groaned, as if recoiling from his presence.

He whispered into the darkness, and the darkness answered. From the edges of the chamber, shapes formed — hunters of shadow, hounds with no flesh, only teeth and eyes that glowed like dying embers.

"They are not prey," the Black Dragon murmured. "They are sparks. And sparks must be smothered before they become flame."

The hounds growled in silence, waiting for the hunt.

The Generals Watch

The Red Dragon scoffed from his place by the shards. "You failed before, shadow. They endured your illusions."

But the Azure Dragon only watched, the mirrored helm tilting. "No — *I* failed. His work is more insidious. Fear lingers long after flame fades."

The Silver Dragon's cruel laughter echoed. "Let him have his chance. Perhaps silence will succeed where fire and trickery did not."

The Shadow Departs

Avarith's voice cut through the chamber once more, low and final. "Do not return without breaking them."

The Black Dragon bowed, his voice a whisper like grinding stone. "They will not die by my hand, my lord. They will *wish* to."

With that, the shadows surged outward, swallowing the chamber. When they cleared, he was gone — a phantom riding the dream-currents, already stalking the Steppe.

Serenya's Warning

In her crystal, Serenya felt the shift — a chill in the dream-currents, colder than any flame, heavier than any illusion. Her fur bristled, her light trembling.

"The shadow moves. He does not come to fight — he comes to break your will. Kaelen... endure. Endure, or you will be lost."

The storm of hooves would soon meet the silence of fear.

Chapter Fifty-Two

The Hunt Begins

Where Fear Finds Its Teeth

The Steppe was quiet. Too quiet.

Kaelen and the others rode under pale moonlight, their horses' hooves striking stone and grass. Ravyn rode ahead, his eyes sharp, but even he could not place the unease that coiled around them.

It began with the wind.

One moment, it blew steady from the east. The next, it shifted without warning, cold as death. The horses stamped and shivered, nostrils flaring.

"Something stalks us," Ravyn muttered.

Kaelorin's blind eyes turned toward the dark. "Not something. *Someone.*"

Whispers in the Night

The shadows lengthened unnaturally. Shapes moved at the edges of vision — men with hollow eyes, wolves with teeth too many, riders long dead.

Lysera gasped, clutching her staff. "I see them... the Steppe Riders. My people. Burned, chained—"

But when Kaelen turned, he saw nothing but shifting shadow.

Then a voice rose among the whispers, cold and venomous:

"You cannot hide. You cannot rest. I will strip you of hope, breath by breath, until you beg for silence."

The Black Dragon.

The Shadow Hounds

From the dark erupted the first strike — hounds made of smoke and ember-eyes, jaws like knives. They leapt silently, their bodies breaking into black mist whenever struck, only to reform again.

Darek cursed, cutting one apart with his blades. "They don't die!"

Kaelen's flame seared one into nothing, but three more rose in its place. Lysera's vines snared them, but the shadows devoured her roots, twisting them black.

Kaelorin's staff shone faintly with starlight, his voice steady. "They are not real. They are *fear* made flesh. Break their hold, not their bodies!"

The General's Gaze

Across the plain, a vast silhouette loomed. The **Black Dragon** himself, half-shrouded in mist, his wings like torn banners of night. His helm burned with two ember-eyes, fixed upon them.

He did not charge. He did not strike. He only watched.

His presence pressed on their hearts like a weight, whispering their failures, showing them visions of betrayals yet to come.

Kaelen staggered, clutching his chest as his flame flickered. Serenya's whisper fought through the storm: *"Endure! He cannot kill you with fear unless you surrender to it!"*

Defiance in the Dark

Kaelen raised his flame high, forcing it brighter than before. "We are not prey!" he shouted, voice cracking through the night.

Ravyn's spear struck the earth, and the horses screamed defiance. Lysera's staff blazed with green light, driving back the hounds. Darek cut through shadow after shadow, refusing to fall.

The Black Dragon hissed, his voice echoing like stone splitting. *"Good. Resist. It makes the breaking sweeter."*

And as suddenly as it had begun, the shadows withdrew, melting into the night.

But his presence lingered. Watching. Hunting.

The Steppe was no longer theirs alone.

Chapter Fifty-Three

Bonds in the Shadow

Where Shadows Cannot Sever

The plain was silent after the attack, save for the ragged breaths of horses and riders alike. The shadows had gone, but their weight lingered, pressing into every heart.

Fear and Doubt

Kaelen stared at his flame, trembling in his palm. It flickered unsteadily, as if reflecting his own shaken spirit. *He hadn't struck. He didn't need to. Just his presence nearly broke us.*

Lysera knelt by the fire, her hands white-knuckled around her staff. "I saw them. My people. Bound. Twisted. As if all I've fought to heal was only a lie." Her voice cracked, but she forced it steady. "What if he's right? What if everything I build crumbles into corruption?"

Darek let out a sharp, bitter laugh, though it rang hollow. "You think that's bad? I saw myself walking away. Leaving you all to die. And the worst part? I believed it. For a moment, I believed that's exactly what I'd do." He gripped his daggers so tightly his knuckles bled.

Even Kaelorin's calm was strained. His blind eyes were tight, his voice low. "He showed me silence. A sky without stars. My life's work, erased. I feared I had guided us into nothingness."

Choosing Defiance

Silence pressed heavy between them. The Black Dragon's whisper still echoed: *"Good. Resist. It makes the breaking sweeter."*

Kaelen clenched his fist, forcing his flame steady. "He wanted us to believe those lies. That's his power. Not claws, not fire—*fear*. He can't break us unless we let him."

Lysera lifted her head, her staff glowing faintly again. "Then we must remind each other what's true."

Darek exhaled hard, wiping blood from his hand. "Fine. Next time he shows me abandoning you, I'll spit in his face and fight twice as hard."

Kaelorin's lips curved into a faint smile. "Fear loses when met with choice. We endure because we choose to."

Strength in Unity

They sat closer around the fire that night, shoulders brushing, their silence no longer empty but shared. Their bond, though shaken, felt stronger — forged not by victory, but by surviving fear together.

Ravyn stood at the edge of the camp, his horse restless beneath the stars. His voice was grim, but steady. "You faced the Black in his own realm. Few can say the same and live. The Steppe Riders learned long ago — the shadow cannot be outrun. It must be met."

Kaelen lifted his flame, holding it against the dark. For the first time since the encounter, it burned steady, bright enough to cast back the shadows.

Serenya's whisper reached them through the dream-currents, warm and fierce:

"Yes. He hunts you. But fear does not chain you. You have chosen defiance — and that is stronger than shadow."

Chapter Fifty-Four

Threads of Treachery

Where Trust Frays, Shadows Feast

The Black Dragon stood alone in a chamber of mirrors, lightless and shifting. The shards of the Eclipsera pulsed around him, feeding his whispers into the dream-currents.

He had tested them with shadows. He had shown them fear. And though they endured, their strength had revealed a deeper target.

"Not their flame. Not their courage," the Black murmured. "Their *trust*. Break their bond, and they will devour themselves."

The Seed of Doubt

He raised his gauntleted hand, shadows spilling between clawed fingers. Within the darkness, shapes formed — Kaelen's flame turning black, Lysera's vines strangling, Darek's blades buried in his allies, Ravyn abandoning them to save only himself.

Each vision sharpened into cruel clarity, not nightmares now but futures — believable, inevitable.

"They trust each other now," the Black hissed, his voice a serpent's coil. "But trust is the most fragile chain. All it takes is one doubt, one hesitation, and the chain breaks."

He wove the visions tighter, twisting them until they carried not only images but *feeling* — suspicion, resentment, betrayal — to slip into his prey's hearts when they least expected.

The Hunters Unleashed

At his feet, shadow-hounds stirred, their ember-eyes burning with hunger. The Black Dragon crouched low, whispering into their ears.

"Do not strike flesh. Strike bond. Drive wedges where their fears are deepest. Let them believe betrayal festers among them, until even their fire burns alone."

The hounds vanished into the dream-currents, carrying seeds of doubt into the Steppe.

The Generals Watch

From the edge of the Spire, the other generals observed. The Azure Dragon's mirrored helm tilted with something like admiration.

"You do not simply kill them," he mused. "You make them kill themselves."

The Red Dragon growled, fists clenched. "Cowardice. If you would end them, strike with fire."

The Black Dragon's ember-eyes flared in the dark. "Your fire leaves scars. My shadow leaves rot. And rot spreads faster than flame."

Serenya's Warning

From within her crystal, Serenya felt the snarl of threads twisting through the dream-currents. Her light trembled as she sensed the seeds of betrayal being sown into her chosen.

Her whisper cut sharp against the dark:

"Kaelen, beware. He hunts not your body, but your bond. Hold fast to one another, or the shadow will tear you apart from within."

The storm would soon face its cruelest trial yet — not against the dragons' blades, but against the fragility of trust.

Chapter Fifty-Five

Fractures in the Flame

When Light Splinters Into Shadow

T he days after the shadow's hunt were quiet. Too quiet. The Steppe stretched wide, its winds whispering across broken plains, but no beast nor arrow disturbed their path. And yet, unease settled in their company like dust that would not be shaken off.

They did not know it yet, but the Black Dragon's poison had already taken root.

Kaelen's Flicker

Kaelen's flame faltered more often than before. When Lysera reached to steady him during practice, he pulled away without meaning to. *She thinks I'm weak,* the thought whispered, unbidden. *She saw how I nearly broke.*

Her look of concern twisted in his mind into judgment, though her words were kind.

Lysera's Doubt

Lysera found herself watching Darek more closely. His blades flashed quick, his eyes always scanning the horizon — but she remembered his confession in the firelight. *"I saw myself leaving you to die."*

Now every time he scouted ahead, the whisper returned: *What if he does? What if he leaves you when it matters most?*

She shook her head, gripping her staff, but the doubt lingered.

Darek's Paranoia

Darek, for his part, caught Kaelen staring at him one night. The boy's flame glowed in his palm, too steady, too focused. Darek felt his skin prickle. *He doesn't trust me,* he thought. *None of them do. Maybe they shouldn't.*

He laughed it off, but his grip on his daggers was tighter, sharper.

Ravyn's Silence

Even Ravyn was not immune. As they rode, he caught Kaelorin murmuring a star-song. To his ears, the words twisted: *"The Steppe rides only to fall again. Your people are already dead."*

Ravyn scowled, turning his gaze away, his chest burning with old scars. He told himself the hermit meant no harm — but the seed had been planted.

The Subtle Drift

They still spoke, still fought side by side, but the rhythm had shifted. Jokes felt hollow. Shared meals passed with longer silences. Glances carried weight they had not before.

The shadow had not struck them with claws or teeth. It did not need to. The doubt it planted grew with every heartbeat, threatening to turn their unity into suspicion.

Far away, in his veil of darkness, the Black Dragon smiled.

Chapter Fifty-Six

Cracks in the Storm

The Tempest Wears Its Wounds

T he companions had ridden hard that day, crossing a barren stretch of the Steppe. By nightfall, exhaustion gnawed at them, and unease pressed thicker than the dust in their lungs.

The silence at their fire was heavy, strained.

Sparks of Distrust

Kaelen watched Darek sharpen his daggers, the sound grating in his ears. *Always ready to draw steel... but against whom?* The whisper in his mind twisted his thoughts: *He'll turn them on you one day.*

Darek caught Kaelen staring. His jaw tightened. "Something on your mind, boy? Or are you just waiting for me to slip?"

Kaelen's flame flared instinctively. "I'm wondering if you're even planning to stay the next time things turn against us."

Darek's blades froze mid-stroke. His eyes narrowed. "You think I'll run?"

Lysera's voice cut sharp, almost panicked. "Enough. This is exactly what he wants—"

But Ravyn's spear struck the ground, his tone hard. "No. Speak it. Better poison spills than festers."

The Boiling Point

Darek rose to his feet, his daggers glinting in the firelight. "I've stayed through fire, shadow, and lies. I could've walked a hundred times, but I didn't. And yet every glance I get from you two is suspicion."

Kaelen stood too, his flame burning bright, defiance in his voice. "Because you admitted it yourself — that you saw yourself leaving us. How do we know you won't?"

Darek's laugh was raw, furious. "I said it because it was *true!* Because the shadow dug up the worst part of me. But if I was going to betray you, Kaelen, you wouldn't wake to see it."

Lysera shoved herself between them, staff glowing. "Stop this! Don't you see? It's not you, it's *him*. The Black Dragon. He wants this!"

But her own voice shook, because the whispers had shown her Darek's betrayal, too.

Kaelorin's Intervention

The blind hermit finally rose, his staff glowing with starlight. His voice was steady, unyielding.

"Listen to yourselves. You doubt not because of truth, but because of fear. That is his weapon. He cannot kill you unless you do it for him."

The fire dimmed, the night air thick with tension. Kaelen's flame wavered, Darek's daggers trembled, Lysera's staff pulsed too bright.

And then Kaelorin slammed his staff down, the light surging between them.

"Decide. Do you choose each other, or do you choose the shadow?"

The Narrow Escape

The silence that followed was unbearable. Then Kaelen forced his flame to dim, his voice breaking. "I choose us."

Darek dropped his daggers with a sharp exhale. "Damn him... I choose us too."

Lysera's shoulders slumped, tears brimming, but she nodded. "Then we hold together. Or we fall."

Ravyn finally spoke, voice like iron. "Good. Because if you'd chosen otherwise, I'd have left you to rot. The Steppe rides only with those who endure."

The tension eased — but barely. The cracks had not closed. They had only been held at bay.

Far away, in the darkness, the Black Dragon's ember-eyes burned. He had not broken them... not yet. But the fissures were there, waiting.

Chapter Fifty-Seven

Ashfang Ambush

Where Silence Ends in Fang and Fire

The fire still smoldered from their argument, the air thick with silence and unspoken doubts. Kaelen sat apart, his flame flickering low. Darek sharpened his daggers with deliberate, angry strokes. Lysera's staff glowed faintly as if she clung to its light to keep her doubts at bay. Ravyn stood watch, his spear planted in the earth, eyes scanning the horizon.

And then the wind shifted.

It carried with it a foul stench — charred flesh and molten glass.

Kaelorin's blind eyes snapped upward. "Something comes."

The Beasts of Fire

The earth split open as **Ashfangs** emerged — beasts twisted by the Red Dragon's fire, half-wolves, half-serpents, their hides cracked with glowing magma. Their maws gushed smoke, their claws burned with ember heat.

A pack of six circled the camp, their growls rumbling like coals in a furnace.

Darek cursed, rising instantly to meet them. "Of course. Right when we're all ready to kill each other anyway."

The lead Ashfang hissed, eyes glowing red. It lunged.

A Battle on the Brink

Kaelen raised his flame, but his focus faltered. His earlier doubts whispered: *What if Darek turns? What if Lysera falters?* The flame wavered, barely striking the beast's flank.

Lysera's vines erupted from the ground, but hesitation slowed her casting, and an Ashfang tore through her defenses, sending her staggering.

Darek fought viciously, blades cutting sparks, but his movements were reckless, fueled by frustration. One slip, and the beast's jaws nearly crushed him.

Even Ravyn struggled to rally them. "Hold your ground! Together, or you'll fall apart!"

But the shadow's poison gnawed at their bond — and the beasts pressed harder.

Choosing Unity

Kaelen fell to his knees as an Ashfang loomed over him. For one terrifying instant, he saw not the beast but Darek's shadow, dagger raised.

And then Lysera screamed, slamming her staff into the ground. Roots surged, pinning the beast long enough for Kaelen to strike. Her eyes locked with his. "Trust me!"

The doubt wavered. His flame surged.

Darek leapt in, finishing the beast with a vicious strike. He turned to Kaelen, chest heaving. "Next time, don't *hesitate!*"

Kaelen swallowed hard, then nodded. "Then don't give me a reason to doubt."

For the first time since the shadow's seeds had been planted, their words held not suspicion but a desperate, fighting trust.

The Turning of the Battle

Ravyn raised his spear high, his horse rearing with a cry. "Riders of the Steppe do not fall to beasts or shadows. Ride with me!"

Something in his voice cut through the doubt. The companions moved as one — Kaelen's flame searing, Lysera's vines binding, Darek's daggers striking true, Ravyn's spear piercing, Kaelorin's star-song steadying.

One by one, the Ashfangs fell, burning to blackened husks in the dust.

When the last beast collapsed, silence fell heavy, broken only by their gasps for breath.

Aftermath

Their wounds were shallow, but the deeper scar was clear. The Black Dragon's shadow still lingered in their hearts.

Kaelen looked around the circle — at Lysera, at Darek, at Ravyn and Kaelorin. He forced his flame steady, raising it high. "We can't let him break us. If we do, every beast, every dragon, every shadow will win before they even strike. We stand, or we fall."

The others met his gaze. Doubt lingered, but so did resolve.

From her crystal, Serenya's whisper carried to them, proud and fierce:

"Yes. You choose each other again. Hold to it — for the shadow will come harder still."

The Steppe was quiet once more, but they all knew: the real hunt had only just begun.

Chapter Fifty-Eight

The Shadow's Fracture

Through the Break, the Light Bleeds

The chamber was drowned in silence. The shards of the Eclipsera pulsed faintly, their fractured glow reflecting off the Black Dragon's armor as he returned from the dream-currents.

He had sown fear. He had turned them against each other. He had watched the cracks spread like veins of rot.

And yet—they endured.

The Black Dragon's Wrath

The shadows around him thickened, twisting into hounds that cowered beneath his fury. His ember-eyes burned like coals in the void.

"They should have broken," he hissed, voice low and venomous. "The boy doubted, the thief raged, the healer faltered, even the Rider's faith wavered. One more breath, one more whisper—and still they clung to one another."

His claws clenched, black steel groaning. "It is not defiance. It is *stubbornness*. Stubbornness can be worn down. They endure today, but tomorrow, they will fracture."

The Generals' Reaction

The Azure Dragon's mirrored helm shimmered with faint amusement. "So. The master of fear finds his prey stronger than expected. Perhaps they are not so easily broken."

The Red Dragon roared with laughter, bitter and cruel. "Your shadows rot, but fire consumes. Give me leave, and I will burn them until even ash denies them comfort."

The Black Dragon turned his helm toward them both, his voice like stone cracking. "Mock me if you wish. But they cannot burn without fire to feed them. They cannot fall to lies if they choose to endure them. But every shadow waits. And shadows are patient."

Avarith's Judgment

The Dark Lord rose from his throne, obsidian armor glowing faintly with veins of molten red. His voice was iron.

"Enough. I do not care for your excuses, shadow. Nor your boasts, flame. Each of you has failed to end them."

His ember gaze narrowed, piercing. "But their unity is not unbreakable. Press harder. Wound deeper. If fear does not shatter them, then fire will. If fire fails, then lies will. They will stumble. They *must*."

Avarith's gauntlet closed around a shard of the Stone, its pulse screaming through the chamber. "Do not return to me with defiance still in their eyes. Break them. Or I will break you."

The Black Dragon bowed low, shadows curling like chains around his form. His voice was steady, but cold with fury.

"They will break, my lord. I swear it."

Serenya's Defiance

In her prison of crystal, Serenya felt the venom of his vow bleed through the dream-currents. The shadows coiled tighter, pressing against her light.

But her sapphire eyes glowed brighter, tails wrapping around her form in defiance.

"No, shadow. They endured you once, and they will again. You cannot unmake trust that has chosen to rise against you. And for every failure of yours, my chains weaken."

The crystal trembled faintly with her whisper. The fox's hope had not been silenced.

Chapter Fifty-Nine

Embers of Trust

In Ash, the Sparks Remain

T he night after the Ashfang ambush was heavy with silence. The
fire burned low, casting long shadows across their camp. No
one spoke at first, each lost in their own thoughts. The air was thick
— not with danger, but with unspoken words.

At last, Kaelen broke it.

Kaelen's Confession

"I doubted you," he said to Darek, his flame flickering weak in his
palm. His voice was hoarse but steady. "When the Black Dragon whispered, I saw you leaving us. I believed it — even when I shouldn't
have."

Darek's jaw tightened. For a long moment, he said nothing. Then he tossed a dagger into the dirt between them and let out a bitter laugh. "Funny. Because I saw myself doing it. Walking away. I thought maybe it was true. Maybe that's all I am."

He looked up, meeting Kaelen's eyes for once without mockery. "But I didn't. I stayed. And I'll keep staying, whether you trust me or not."

Kaelen clenched his fist. "Then I'll choose to trust. Even when it's hard."

Lysera's Fear

Lysera's staff glowed faintly, her knuckles white around it. "I saw myself killing you," she whispered. Her voice trembled, but she forced the words out. "My roots, my healing, twisted into poison. I feared that's all I am — someone who only brings ruin."

Kaelen reached for her hand, his flame warming her fingers. "Your gift saved me more times than I can count. The Black Dragon twisted it, but I won't let him twist how I see you. And neither should you."

Her eyes brimmed with tears, but her grip tightened around his hand.

Ravyn and Kaelorin

Ravyn stood apart, spear planted in the earth. His voice was low, hard as stone. "The shadow showed me my people's death again. And worse — that all of this, all of you, is just another doomed banner. I wanted to believe it. Easier than hoping again."

Kaelorin lifted his staff, its faint starlight glowing against the dark. "Hope is never easier. But it is always worth the burden. The shadow fears hope more than fire, more than steel. That is why he strikes it first."

Ravyn's eyes lingered on the hermit, then on the group. At last, he gave a slow nod. "Then I'll bear it. Even if it breaks me."

The Oath of the Steppe

Ravyn stepped closer, raising his spear. "The Steppe Riders once swore an oath: *Ride not for yourself, but for those beside you.* If you falter, remember that oath. If you doubt, remember it. Because the shadow will not stop. He'll whisper again, and louder. Only by holding fast to each other will you endure."

One by one, they placed their hands upon the spear — Kaelen's flame, Lysera's staff, Darek's blades, Kaelorin's starlight.

Together, they spoke, voices unsteady but united:

"We endure."

The fire flared bright, burning shadows back into the night.

From her crystal, Serenya's whisper carried to them, warm with pride:

"Yes. This is your strength. Not flame, not steel, not magic — but choice. And so long as you choose each other, the shadow cannot win."

The cracks in their bond had not vanished, but they had begun to mend. And this time, they mended stronger.

Chapter Sixty

Roads Toward the Shard

Every Path Converges on the Broken Light

The dawn after their oath rose quiet and clear, the Steppe winds softer, as if even the land itself acknowledged their choice. Their unity had been shaken, but not shattered. And now, the road pulled them onward — toward the next shard of the Eclipsera Stone.

The Lore of the Next Shard

As they rode, Kaelorin spoke, his voice low but sure.
"The shards call to one another. Even broken, they yearn to be whole.

The flame you carry, Kaelen, burns brighter when you near another piece. That is both strength — and danger."

Ravyn glanced at him, eyes sharp. "And where does this next shard lie?"

Kaelorin tilted his head skyward, listening to currents unseen. "North, beyond the Steppe. In the ruins of a drowned citadel — **Veyra's Fall.** A city once lifted high by sorcery, until the dragons cast it down into the sea."

Lysera frowned. "A drowned citadel? How can we reach it?"

Kaelorin smiled faintly. "Not all of it sleeps beneath the waves. The highest spires still pierce the surface. But the shard will not lie in light. It waits in the deepest chambers below."

The Journey North

They pressed onward, leaving the endless plains behind. The land grew harsher: cliffs of black stone, rivers carved deep into the earth, storms rolling heavy from the northern sea. Their horses labored, and every step felt heavier with the shard's growing pull.

Kaelen felt it most — the shard in his hand pulsing faintly, like a heartbeat answering a distant call. Each night, his dreams burned with glimpses of the drowned city: shattered towers, halls choked with water, shadows moving in the deep.

The Weight of What's Coming

Around their fires, talk grew quieter. Ravyn sharpened his spear, eyes on the horizon. Darek twirled his daggers, restless but more thoughtful than mocking. Lysera tended the horses with tired hands, her healing drained but still offered freely.

Kaelen watched them, flame flickering steady in his palm. Despite everything — the doubts, the fear, the shadow — they were still here. Still enduring.

And yet, as the wind carried the scent of salt and storm, he knew: the drowned citadel would test them in ways shadow and fire had not.

Serenya's whisper came to him that night, softer than before, almost mournful:

"The sea hides many things, Kaelen. Not only shards — but truths buried too long. Be ready, for what lies beneath may change you."

The road stretched onward, and the sea awaited.

Chapter Sixty-One

The Road of Storms

When Lightning Marks the Way

T he further north they rode, the harsher the land became. The Steppe gave way to jagged ridges of black stone, rivers swollen with storm-runoff, and skies heavy with the scent of salt and lightning.

The shard in Kaelen's hand pulsed stronger each day, its heartbeat answering the call of something buried beneath the waves. And with each pulse, unease grew among them.

The Omen in the Sky

One night, as they made camp near a wind-carved gorge, the sky split open. Lightning arced not white, but *violet*, striking again and again in the same place on the northern horizon.

Ravyn's horse stamped and snorted nervously, and even the Steppe Rider's calm eyes flickered with unease.

"That storm is not natural," he muttered. "No wind moves like that."

Kaelorin tilted his blind eyes upward, his voice low. "Not storm, but sign. The sea itself resists what lies within it. The shard's corruption seeps outward... twisting sky and tide alike."

The Harbinger

As they watched, a flock of seabirds flew overhead — only to suddenly twist mid-flight, plummeting into the earth as if struck by an unseen force. Their bodies hit the ground around the camp, lifeless, eyes glassy and black.

Lysera knelt beside one, her hand trembling as she brushed its feathers. "They didn't fall by chance. Something *pulled* them down."

The shard in Kaelen's palm pulsed violently, his flame flaring in answer. His chest tightened. "It's calling. And whatever lies in Veyra's Fall... it doesn't want to be found."

Resolve in the Face of Dread

Darek spat into the dirt, shaking his head. "Great. Birds falling from the sky. The sea trying to kill us before we even see it. At this rate, we'll drown before we touch the water."

But Ravyn's voice cut through his cynicism, sharp and iron. "No. If the land and sky rise against us, then it means the shard fears us. And if it fears us, we cannot turn back."

Kaelen clenched the shard tighter, flame steady despite the storm pulsing inside him. "Then forward. Whatever waits in that drowned city, we'll face it together."

Serenya's whisper brushed faintly against his heart, fierce despite the dread that weighed on her words:

"Yes. Do not waver. But beware... for beneath the waves, not all shadows come from the Black Dragon."

The road narrowed, the storm ahead grew louder, and the sea drew near.

Chapter Sixty-Two

The Drowned Spires

The Depths Remember What Stood Above

T he air turned briny long before the sea came into view. The wind carried salt and storm, heavy with a scent of decay. Waves boomed in the distance, growing louder with each mile until the companions crested the final ridge.

There it was.

The Storm-Lashed Coast

The sea spread wide and black beneath a sky torn with violet lightning. Jagged cliffs plunged into crashing waves, spray leaping high as if the ocean itself tried to claw the land apart.

And far beyond the breakers, half-submerged in the furious water, the drowned citadel revealed itself.

Veyra's Fall

Shattered spires jutted from the sea like broken teeth, their tops leaning, their stone slick with centuries of storm. Once, they must have been magnificent — towers of pale marble, etched with runes that even now faintly glowed through the mist. But the city's foundations had been ripped from beneath it, cast down into the abyss by dragon wrath.

Only fragments remained above the surface. The rest slumbered below, waiting in the crushing dark.

Kaelen felt the shard in his palm pulse violently, his flame guttering in response. "It's here. I can feel it... beneath the waves."

The Weight of Dread

Lysera shivered, clutching her staff tighter. "How can we reach it? That storm alone could tear us apart."

Ravyn frowned, his spear planted in the sand. "The Steppe Riders knew of the sea, but we never rode it. This is not a battlefield of hooves or wind."

Darek spat into the foam. "Figures. We just survived fire, shadow, illusions, and an army of beasts... and now we're supposed to dive into a cursed ruin at the bottom of the sea."

Kaelorin's blind eyes lifted toward the distant spires, his voice grave. "The shard's pull is stronger here than anywhere we have walked. But shards corrupt what they touch. If it waits below, it will not be unguarded."

Serenya's Whisper

Kaelen felt the fox's whisper stir within him, faint but insistent, carried on the roar of the waves.

"Be wary. What sleeps beneath the sea is not only dragon's ruin — but ancient sorrow. The citadel fell not by fire alone. And some who drowned with it never left."

The companions stood together on the storm-lashed shore, staring at the broken city of Veyra's Fall. The next shard awaited them — but so did whatever horrors the deep still held.

Chapter Sixty-Three

Before the Descent

The Last Light Before the Fall

T he storm hammered the coast, waves crashing hard against the jagged cliffs. The drowned spires of Veyra's Fall loomed in the distance, half-hidden by mist and lightning. The shard's pull grew stronger with every heartbeat, and the companions knew the time had come.

But none of them rushed forward. The sea demanded caution.

Gathering What They Could

Ravyn led them down the shoreline, where wrecks of ships lay splintered among the rocks. From the remains they scavenged rope, rusted hooks, and shattered boards. Darek cursed at the condition of the gear, but still bound together a makeshift harness of leather and rope.

"If we're going under," he said, "we're not trusting the sea to be kind. Tie together, and if one falls, the others drag him back."

Lysera found reeds and hollow driftwood, fashioning crude breath-tubes. She tested them in the shallows, surfacing with salt-stung eyes. "Not perfect, but enough to hold air for moments longer. Enough to make the difference between drowning and breathing."

Kaelen tested his flame against the storm. It sputtered, hissed, but did not die. He clenched his fist. "It won't burn bright under the waves, but it will burn. That has to be enough."

The Weighing of Doubts

That night, they huddled in a cave for shelter. The roar of the sea filled the silence, relentless and merciless.

Darek spoke first, his voice low. "I've slit a dozen purses, outrun a hundred guards. But swimming into a graveyard full of drowned towers? Feels like suicide."

Lysera met his gaze, her voice calm but weary. "Everything we've done has felt like suicide. And yet... we're still here."

Kaelorin sat apart, tracing constellations in the sand though no stars pierced the storm. His voice was heavy. "The sea is memory. It swallows what was, buries it, makes it eternal. But the shard's corruption twists that memory. We will not only face water and ruin... but ghosts of what drowned there."

Ravyn's spear gleamed faintly in the firelight. His words were iron. "Then we ride the storm as we ride the Steppe. Head unbowed. Fear will not drag us down."

Serenya's Whisper

As Kaelen drifted into uneasy sleep, the fox's voice reached him, clearer than before despite the storm.

"Be wary, Kaelen. The sea drowns more than flesh — it drowns truth. What you see below may not be lies, but pieces of what was, twisted by sorrow. Trust yourself. Trust them. Or the deep will claim you."

Kaelen woke with the shard pulsing hot in his hand. The others stirred around him, restless, each carrying their own fears into dawn.

Tomorrow, they would descend into the drowned citadel. And whatever awaited them beneath the storm-lashed waves would test them in ways shadow and fire never had.

Chapter Sixty-Four

Into the Teeth of the Sea

The Abyss Opens Its Maw

The morning broke gray, the storm unyielding. The drowned spires loomed in the mist like broken spears, waiting.

The companions stood at the edge of the coast, ropes bound, makeshift rafts lashed from wreckage scavenged the night before. The sea roared like a beast, waves shattering against the cliffs as though to warn them back.

And still, they pushed forward.

The Launch

Ravyn shoved the raft into the surf, his spear serving as both pole and weapon. "No wave is too fierce for those who ride together," he growled. "Row with me, or drown."

Kaelen leapt aboard, flame guttering against the spray. Lysera followed, staff glowing faintly green as she whispered protective wards into the reeds. Darek shoved from behind, muttering curses as salt stung his eyes. Kaelorin was last, calm even as the sea raged, his blind eyes lifted toward the storm.

The raft bucked immediately, nearly tossing them into the foam.

Battle with the Waves

The sea struck them in relentless fury. A wave surged, high as a wall, slamming the raft sideways. Kaelen's flame burst bright, forcing back the surge just enough for Ravyn to steer into it.

Another wave hurled driftwood like spears. Lysera raised her staff, roots sprouting in a sudden lattice to shield them — but the effort drained her, and she nearly collapsed into Kaelen's arms.

Darek lashed rope around them all, teeth gritted. "If one goes in, we *all* go in. That way no one dies alone!"

Spray blinded them, thunder split the sky, and lightning struck so close the sea itself turned white.

Wreckage and Ghosts

Amid the storm, shapes floated in the water — not driftwood, but wrecks of old ships. Smashed hulls, broken masts, and corpses long drowned tangled in seaweed. Their eyeless faces turned toward the raft as the waves rolled them near.

Lysera's breath caught. "They were part of Veyra's fall... still trapped in its ruin."

One of the corpses reached for the raft, mouth opening in a soundless scream. Kaelen seared it away with fire, but the image lingered in all their minds.

First Sight of the Spires

At last, between the crash of waves, the drowned city broke through the mist. Towers jutted from the black water, their tops fractured, their walls etched with runes glowing faintly violet. The storm seemed to circle the ruins, drawn to them, as though the city itself bled corruption into the sky.

The shard in Kaelen's hand pulsed so violently he nearly dropped it. His flame flared in answer, bright even against the storm. "It's there," he gasped. "Beneath it. Waiting."

Ravyn braced his spear against the raft, eyes fixed forward. "Then we ride into the storm. No turning back."

Serenya's Whisper

Her voice reached Kaelen through the roar of waves, faint but burning.

"Be strong. The sea tests not your body, but your will. Trust in them, as they must trust in you — or the depths will claim you all."

Together, the companions steered their fragile raft into the drowned spires of Veyra's Fall.

The descent awaited.

Chapter Sixty-Five

The Spires Above

Above the Storm, Secrets Endure

The raft drifted into the labyrinth of broken towers. The storm pressed harder here, waves slamming against marble walls slick with moss and salt. Jagged spires leaned toward one another, forming arches half-submerged, as if the city still clung to dignity even in ruin.

But dignity had long since drowned.

The First Guardians

Shapes moved among the waves. At first, Kaelen thought they were driftwood, but then the forms rose — pale, bloated, armored in rust and seaweed. Figures that had once been Veyran soldiers, their faces gray and eyeless, their mouths dripping brine.

Lysera gasped, clutching her staff. "They're not alive..."

Kaelorin's blind eyes darkened. "No. Bound by the shard's corruption. Drowned souls, tethered to their ruin."

One lurched onto the raft with unnatural speed, its rusted blade screeching against Darek's daggers. Another clawed at Lysera's warding vines, hissing water from its throat. More shadows moved in the waves — dozens of them, circling like sharks.

The Battle on the Surface

Kaelen's flame hissed as he struck, the sea trying to smother it, but his fire still burned bright enough to scorch the drowned soldier's chest. It staggered, fell back into the waves, but three more climbed to take its place.

Darek cursed, cutting through rotted sinew and rusted armor. "They just keep coming!"

Ravyn's spear flashed, driving one back into the depths. "They'll swarm until we fall! Cut a path — *forward!*"

Lysera raised her staff, roots bursting from cracks in the marble spires, snaring drowned warriors long enough to topple them back into the sea. But each spell drained her faster, her voice breaking as she cried, "There are too many!"

The Shard's Call

Kaelen staggered, the shard in his hand pulsing violently, almost dragging him toward the waves. Visions blurred his sight — drowned halls below, treasure and terror alike. And a voice, whispering through the foam:

"Come down. Join us. Be part of what was lost."

He clenched his jaw, forcing the flame brighter. "No. I am not yours."

But the shard's hunger grew, tugging at his will even as the drowned guardians closed in.

Serenya's Warning

Her voice cut through the roar of waves and screams, sharp and urgent:

"Kaelen! The shard reaches for you, but it cannot take you unless you yield. Remember who you are. Remember who rides with you!"

The flame steadied in his palm, burning back the water that sought to drown it. He lifted it high, its light cutting through the storm. The drowned guardians shrieked, recoiling as though seared by truth itself.

The raft surged forward, breaking free of the swarm. But the drowned spires loomed taller around them, and below... the true citadel waited.

The surface was only the beginning.

Chapter Sixty-Six

Into the Deep

Where Light Yields to Silence

T he raft scraped against the marble of a leaning spire, wedged in a hollow between ruined walls. The storm still raged above, but here the water surged calmer, as if drawing them downward.

Ravyn tied the ropes around them all, his voice hard. "Stay bound. If the sea takes one of us, the others drag them back."

Darek muttered, tugging his knots tight. "Great comfort, drowning together."

Kaelen lifted the shard, its pulse wild, pulling him toward the depths. The flame in his palm hissed as seawater licked at it, but still it burned. "It's below. Waiting."

Lysera clutched her reed-breathing tube, staff glowing faintly. "Then we go."

Kaelorin placed his hand on the rope that bound them, blind eyes serene. "The stars cannot guide us here. Trust your bond instead."

The Descent Begins

One by one, they plunged into the water.

The cold struck instantly — a crushing embrace that tore the air from their lungs and replaced it with salt and silence. The rope strained between them as they sank, bubbles streaming upward, the drowned spires stretching tall around them.

Light faded quickly. Kaelen's flame flickered in his palm, the only beacon. It cast eerie shadows across broken arches, shattered bridges, and statues of kings long drowned.

The Drowned City

As they descended, the city revealed itself — plazas half-buried in silt, towers tipped on their sides, banners turned to tatters of seaweed. Schools of pale fish darted through broken windows, scattering as the companions passed.

But the deeper they sank, the stranger it became. Runes carved into marble still glowed faint violet, pulsing in rhythm with the shard Kaelen carried. Some doors were barred by chains of light that flickered and twisted like living things.

And always, from the abyss below, something whispered.

"Come deeper... join us... drown with us..."

First Contact

Lysera's eyes widened as she pointed into the gloom. Shapes moved —
too large to be fish. Warriors in armor floated upright, drifting silently,
their helmets turned toward the intruders. Their mouths opened,
spilling streams of bubbles like broken prayers.

Darek tightened his grip on his daggers, teeth gritted.

The drowned guardians were waiting for them.

And below, the shard's call grew stronger.

Chapter Sixty-Seven

The Drowned Host

The Sea Remembers Every Soldier

The drowned soldiers drifted forward, silent as the grave. Rusted helms turned toward the intruders, their eyeless faces spilling streams of bubbles. Chains of seaweed clung to their limbs, but their movements were swift, purposeful, inexorable.

The companions tightened their grips on rope and weapon alike. Even in the crushing silence, the tension roared.

And then the first guardian lunged.

Clash Beneath the Waves

Kaelen's flame burst in his palm, fire hissing in water but still burning with furious light. He drove it into the guardian's chest — steam erupted, bubbles boiling — but the corpse fought on, dragging him down with ironclad arms.

Darek cut the rope loose between them in a heartbeat, diving in with flashing daggers. He drove one blade between rusted plates, tearing the corpse back, bubbles rising in a crimson cloud. His grin was grim. *Even here, steel finds a throat.*

Lysera's staff glowed green, vines of kelp bursting from the stone below. They coiled around two guardians at once, dragging them to the silt. But as her roots tightened, their eyeless faces turned to her, mouths opening in silent wails. She shuddered, nearly losing her focus as the kelp blackened with corruption.

Ravyn speared through one guardian's helm, the shock of impact shuddering down his arms. The corpse fell still, but another rose behind it. His horse was not here — only the strength of his lungs, his fury, and his oath.

Kaelorin's crystal staff glimmered faint starlight, the glow guiding the others even in the gloom. He raised his voice in a wordless hum, a resonance that rippled through the water. The drowned warriors faltered, slowed — memory stirring in their corrupted forms.

The Shard's Temptation

Even as they fought, the shard in Kaelen's hand pulsed harder, pulling him deeper. Visions flooded his mind — drowned halls, treasures gleaming, voices of the dead calling his name. His flame flickered.

"Come to us, Kaelen," the whispers breathed through the water. *"Burn for us, as we drowned for you."*

He faltered, and a guardian's blade nearly pierced his chest before Lysera's vines yanked it aside. Her eyes burned through the water: *Trust me.*

The flame steadied. He roared bubbles into the deep, driving fire into the guardian's helm until it shattered.

Turning the Tide

Together, they pressed back — Kaelen's fire searing, Lysera's roots binding, Darek's daggers flashing, Ravyn's spear driving, Kaelorin's light guiding.

The drowned host shrieked silently as their bodies unraveled, breaking into brine and shadow, dissolving into the currents.

When the last corpse fell, silence returned — heavier, deeper.

The companions clung to the rope, lungs burning, hearts pounding. The battle had been won. But below them, darker shapes stirred in the abyss — larger, older.

And the shard's call had only grown stronger.

Chapter Sixty-Eight

The Halls Below

Beneath the World, the Past Endures

T he last bubbles of the drowned guardians drifted upward, leaving only silence and the pulse of the shard in Kaelen's hand. The rope binding them tugged faintly as Ravyn pointed down into the abyss.

"Deeper," he signaled with a sharp gesture. "The shard lies below." And so they dove.

Into the Abyss

Light vanished quickly as they descended past shattered balconies and toppled spires, broken murals half-consumed by coral. Statues of forgotten kings loomed from the dark, their faces eroded to grim masks. The weight of the sea pressed harder with every stroke.

Kaelen's flame flickered but endured, casting just enough glow to show their path. Lysera's vines trailed faintly in the current, brushing stone walls for anchorage. Darek kicked hard against the pull of the deep, daggers still in hand as if he would cut the water itself if it tried to bind him. Ravyn's spear glimmered like a guiding line, and Kaelorin's faint hum steadied their hearts against the oppressive silence.

The Halls of the Drowned

They passed through an archway of cracked marble, runes glowing faint violet, into a vast hall. Once it might have been a throne room — pillars carved with spirals rose from the floor, banners now only tatters drifting like ghosts.

The throne itself lay toppled, half-buried in silt. And at its base, a massive chain of light bound something beneath the floor, pulsing in rhythm with the shard Kaelen carried.

The shard in his hand burned hot, its pulse wild. *"Closer,"* the whisper urged. *"Just a little deeper. Take me back to myself."*

Kaelen's breath caught, bubbles streaming past his lips. His hand trembled, almost reaching—

The Guardians Awaken

A sudden shudder rippled through the hall. The silt rose in clouds, obscuring sight. From the shadows between the pillars, more forms emerged — larger than the drowned soldiers above.

Knights in blackened armor, their helms crowned with barnacle and coral. Their weapons were not rusted blades but spears of jagged bone, still glowing with faint sorcery. They moved as one, their eyes burning faint violet.

Kaelorin's hum broke into sharp warning. He pointed his staff toward them, bubbles rushing from his mouth. **"They guard it."**

The drowned knights advanced, the entire hall shifting as if the sea itself were their ally.

Serenya's Whisper

Through the water, faint but piercing, Serenya's voice reached Kaelen:

"This is the heart of Veyra's sorrow. Do not let it drown you. Trust your flame, trust each other — or the sea will claim you forever."

Kaelen's flame burst brighter in the dark. His companions gathered close, bound by rope and by will, as the drowned knights closed in.

The shard pulsed wildly beneath the throne — waiting, watching.

And the true battle of Veyra's Fall was about to begin.

Chapter Sixty-Nine

Silent Resolve

The Still Flame That Will Not Break

The drowned throne hall was a cathedral of shadows, pillars rising into blackness, runes burning faint on the walls. The knights drifted forward with the inevitability of the tide, bone spears glinting faint violet. The sea pressed heavy, every heartbeat a struggle for breath.

Bound by their rope, the companions paused. For a moment, there was no clash — only the shared stillness before violence.

Kaelen

Kaelen's flame guttered in his palm, a beacon in the dark. He could feel the shard's pull in his chest, dragging him toward the chained throne, promising power and release. *If I reach it, this ends. But if I lose myself to it... we all drown.*

He looked to his friends, forcing the flame steadier. He lifted his hand, signaling: **Hold together. Don't break.**

Lysera

Lysera's staff glowed faint green, but fear coiled in her chest. The drowned knights had been people once — guardians, defenders of their home. Corrupted now into weapons for a shard's hunger. She prayed her magic could bind without destroying, but the sea whispered: *All you touch will rot.*

She shook her head violently, pushing the whisper away. Meeting Kaelen's eyes, she touched her chest, then spread her fingers outward — **I trust.**

Darek

Darek's daggers gleamed in the flame's glow. He hated the silence of water — no sound of blades striking, no satisfying cry of victory. Only the crushing quiet. He remembered the shadow's whisper of betrayal, and for a breath it almost returned. *Why not leave them here, take the shard yourself?*

But then Lysera's trust-sign cut through the fog, and he spat a stream of bubbles, baring his teeth at the knights. He gave Kaelen a sharp nod and tapped his dagger to his heart — **I stay.**

Ravyn

The Rider shifted his spear, anchoring himself against the pull of the sea. To ride the Steppe was to ride storms, but this... this was a storm without wind. His people's oath echoed: *Ride not for yourself, but for those beside you.*

He pointed his spear forward, signaling with fierce certainty: **Strike first. Break their line.**

Kaelorin

The hermit's blind eyes closed, his staff glowing faintly like starlight even beneath the waves. He heard the drowned knights' sorrow, a dirge in the deep. Fear gnawed at him — that his voice would not reach his companions here, that his wisdom would drown unheeded.

But Kaelen's flame touched his hand in the rope-chain, steady and warm. Kaelorin hummed softly, the resonance vibrating through the water into each of them. No words, only resolve: **You are not alone.**

The Moment Before

They looked to one another, signals passed through flame, staff, steel, spear, and song. Doubt lingered, fear pressed, but trust — fragile yet chosen — bound them stronger than rope.

The drowned knights closed in, violet eyes burning through the dark.

Kaelen raised his flame high.

And the battle began.

Chapter Seventy

Fury in the Deep

Where Silence Breaks into Storm

The drowned knights surged forward, bone spears gleaming with violet light, their movements swift and merciless despite centuries beneath the waves. The hall shook as if the sea itself struck with them.

Bound together by rope and trust, the companions answered in kind.

Kaelen — Fire Against the Sea

Kaelen thrust his flame forward, his palm blazing in defiance of the ocean's choke. The water hissed and boiled around him, steam erupting as his fire clashed against the knights' spears. Every strike drained him, but the flame *burned*, refusing to die even beneath the sea.

One knight's weapon pierced his shoulder — Kaelen gritted his teeth, flame erupting from the wound itself, searing through the knight's helm until it dissolved into shadow and brine.

"You will not drown me," he thought, pushing his fire brighter.

Lysera — Binding Life to Death

Lysera's staff pulsed green, roots bursting even here, kelp twisting alive at her command. She wrapped them around two knights at once, their armor grinding as they were pulled to the floor. For a moment, she thought she had bound them — until their violet eyes flared, the kelp blackening into ash in her hands.

Her heart trembled. *Am I only feeding their corruption?*

But Kaelen's flame brushed her vines, searing the corruption away. Lysera's eyes widened — her roots glowed green again, alive. She smiled through the salt, her staff burning brighter.

Darek — Steel in the Dark

Darek spun through the water like a shadow himself, daggers flashing silver. He cut ropes of seaweed, severed joints in rusted armor, and tore through the drowned with savage precision. His lungs screamed for air, but his fury carried him forward.

One knight seized him by the throat, dragging him down. Darek's vision blurred, salt choking him — until Ravyn's spear impaled the knight through the chest, pinning it to the floor. Darek spat a stream of bubbles, flashing a wolfish grin of thanks before spinning back into the fight.

Ravyn — The Rider Without a Horse

The Rider moved like a storm, his spear a blur of motion even in the deep. He drove through the knights' line, scattering them, his strikes punctuated by the sharp glint of his eyes. Though no hooves thundered here, his movements carried the rhythm of the Steppe — relentless, unbroken.

He struck one knight's helm free, the face beneath nothing but bone and coral. Ravyn spat a trail of bubbles, spear raised again. *"Even drowned, you cannot stand against the storm."*

Kaelorin — The Star's Song

Kaelorin's staff shone faint starlight, his blind eyes closed, his hum resonating through the water. The sound rippled into the drowned knights, slowing their strikes, unsettling their corrupted rhythm.

For a moment, Kaelen thought he saw — through Kaelorin's song — the men these knights had once been. Guardians, proud, sworn to protect. Now broken into weapons of the shard. His flame burned hotter, mourning them even as he destroyed them.

Breaking the Line

Together, they tore through the drowned host. Rope bound them, but trust carried them. Fire seared, vines bound, daggers cut, spear drove, and starlight guided. One by one, the knights dissolved into brine and shadow, their violet eyes flickering out.

At last, only silence remained. The throne hall shook, chains of light binding the floor pulsing brighter. The shard's call thundered in Kaelen's chest, dragging his flame toward it.

The true heart of Veyra's Fall waited beneath.

Chapter
Seventy-One

The Weight of
Silence

The Stillness That Cracks the Soul

T he last drowned knight dissolved into shadow and silt. The hall
was still again, save for the slow drift of bubbles and the faint
pulse of runes on the cracked marble.

The companions floated in the water, bound together by rope and
exhaustion, each fighting the urge to collapse into the depths.

Kaelen

His flame dimmed to a trembling ember, barely holding against the sea. His shoulder bled sluggishly where the spear had pierced, his breath burned in his lungs. Yet the shard still pulsed in his palm, pulling harder than ever.

Closer... deeper...

He clenched his fist against it. "Not yet," he thought. "Not until we're ready."

Lysera

Her staff quivered with drained magic. The kelp she'd conjured had turned black under the shard's touch — it still haunted her, the thought that her gift might twist into poison again. She pressed her free hand to the rope linking them. Kaelen's warmth pulsed faintly through it.

"I trust," she mouthed through the bubbles, needing him to know.

Darek

Darek's daggers still gleamed with the last remnants of battle. He wanted to grin, to boast that even the sea couldn't stop him — but his chest burned, his lungs screamed, and he'd nearly drowned when that knight had dragged him down.

One slip, and I'd be gone, he thought bitterly. *And they'd have to carry my weight to the bottom.*

He closed his eyes, then gave a sharp tug on the rope. A silent signal to the others: **Still here. Not leaving.**

Ravyn

The Rider's spear hovered steady, though his arm shook from the strain. He had no horse here, no Steppe beneath him, but his oath burned bright even in the dark. He watched Kaelen, Lysera, Darek — each faltering, each enduring.

"The Steppe rides with them," he thought grimly. "And so do I."

Kaelorin

The hermit floated still, staff glowing faintly, his blind eyes closed. His hum resonated in the water, soft and steady, a reminder they were not alone. He had seen flashes in the fight — glimpses of the guardians' old vows, their sorrow bound into chains.

"They were protectors once," he thought. "And in destroying them, we freed them."

The Hall Waits

The throne loomed ahead, toppled, chained with glowing light. The shard pulsed beneath it, calling, promising, hungering.

But for a moment longer, the companions held still — bound not just by rope, but by the choice they had made again and again: to endure, together.

Serenya's whisper drifted through the currents, softer than before, but fierce with pride:

"Yes. Rest, even in the deep. For what waits below will test you greater still. And only those who trust may rise from it."

The silence of the drowned hall held them close, heavy with the weight of what had been lost — and what they must now face.

Chapter
Seventy-Two

Chains of the
Deep

The Weight That Drowns the Soul

The throne lay toppled and half-buried in silt, its marble cracked, its gilding dulled to black. But what drew every gaze were the chains — massive lengths of glowing light, not metal but woven runes, binding the base of the throne to the floor.

The shard's pulse throbbed from beneath, beating against the bindings like a heart trying to tear free.

The First Attempts

Kaelen drifted closer, flame flickering in his palm. He pressed it against the chain. The fire hissed and flared, but the runes only burned brighter, feeding on his flame instead of weakening. He yanked his hand back, teeth clenched. "It drinks fire."

Darek scowled, pulling a dagger free. "Then let's see how it likes steel." He slashed — sparks erupted in the water, the dagger's edge ringing against the glowing links. The blade cracked down the middle. He swore a stream of bubbles, fury in his eyes. "Steel's useless."

Lysera raised her staff, green light blossoming through the water. Vines curled out, wrapping around the chain. For a moment, it seemed the bindings trembled — until the light warped sickly, her vines withering black in her grip. She gasped, staggering back into Kaelen's steadying hand.

Ravyn's Insight

Ravyn circled the throne, spear probing the silt around the base. His eyes narrowed. "It's not just a chain. It's a ward. A lock."

He gestured sharply. **Not brute force. Break the pattern.**

Kaelorin's blind eyes turned toward the rune-light. He placed his palm against the chain, staff glowing faintly. "Yes. This is not meant to hold the shard for us. It was meant to bind it *forever*. Veyra's last defenders chained their ruin, to keep the shard from rising again."

A Heavy Choice

The companions exchanged glances.

Lysera signed through the rope: **If we break it, we free the shard's corruption.**

Kaelen's flame flared. **If we leave it, we cannot mend the Stone.**

Ravyn gripped his spear tighter. "Then we break it. But we must be ready for what crawls out."

Darek gave a sharp nod, teeth bared. "Fine. Let's cut it loose — and kill whatever comes crawling."

Kaelorin's hum deepened, the starlight in his staff glowing brighter. "Then strike not with strength, but with harmony. Fire, root, steel, spear, and star together. The chains can only break if we stand as one."

Serenya's Whisper

The fox's voice carried faint but steady through the crushing water:

"Yes. Strike together. As they chained it with unity, so only unity can unbind. But beware — what they bound was not the shard alone."

The companions tightened their grips — on rope, on weapon, on each other.

And as one, they prepared to strike at the chains of the drowned throne.

Chapter
Seventy-Three

The Shard
Unbound

Where Balance Shatters, Shadows Rise

The companions formed a circle around the throne's base, their rope taut, each one gripping staff, blade, flame, or spear. The glowing chains pulsed with runic light, thrumming like a heartbeat that was not their own. The shard's pull grew wild, almost frantic, as if it knew freedom was close.

Kaelorin's hum deepened, resonating through the water, guiding their rhythm. His voice was steady, unwavering.

"Now. Together."

The Strike of Unity

Kaelen thrust his flame forward, blue fire searing against the rune-light.

Lysera's staff blazed green, vines and kelp surging, binding the chain.

Darek's daggers struck in sharp arcs, steel flashing.

Ravyn's spear drove down like a storm breaking stone.

Kaelorin's staff released a burst of starlight, the song of the heavens itself piercing the deep.

Their powers converged as one, a storm of fire, root, steel, spear, and star colliding with the luminous bindings.

For a moment, the chains resisted — the runes flared, brighter and brighter, fighting their unity with ancient fury.

Then came the fracture.

A crack split through the light, violet shards scattering into the water like glass. With a thunderous pulse, the chains shattered, dissolving into the depths.

The Release

The throne groaned, toppling fully into the silt. From beneath it, the shard rose — a jagged crystal of violet and azure, its glow harsh, alive, screaming. The sea quaked, bubbles rushing upward in a torrent.

But it was not alone.

From the broken floor beneath, something vast stirred.

The Bound Guardian

A colossal shape emerged — not a knight, not a soldier, but the **drowned king** himself. His crown was fused with coral, his body a husk wrapped in barnacle and rune-fire. Chains still clung to his limbs, broken but writhing like serpents, their light feeding him. His eyes burned with the shard's violet glow.

The sea churned around him as he rose, towering over the companions.

Kaelen's flame flickered in his palm. The shard pulsed wild in his grasp, almost tearing free.

Serenya's whisper reached them, sharp with warning:

"They did not only bind the shard — they bound him to it. And now he is free."

The drowned king raised his shattered scepter, the water itself bending at his command.

And the true trial of Veyra's Fall began.

Chapter
Seventy-Four

The Drowned
King's Shadow

The Throne That Sinks, Yet Rules Still

The throne cracked apart, sinking into the silt. The shard's glow flared like a starburst, violet and azure light tearing through the water. From the rubble, the colossal figure rose — the **drowned king**, bound and yet unbound, his ruined crown fused with coral, his eyes blazing with the shard's fire.

The sea itself bowed to his presence, currents bending at the wave of his shattered scepter.

The Weight of What They Unleashed

Kaelen's flame faltered as he stared upward at the giant's form. The shard in his palm throbbed like a heartbeat that wasn't his own, trying to tear free, to answer the king's call. His stomach sank.
We freed it. We freed him.

Lysera's breath hitched, her staff trembling. "The guardians we fought... they weren't enough. This was what they were binding. Their king, twisted to serve the shard."

Ravyn bared his teeth, spear gripped tight. For a moment, even he looked small against the figure looming over them. "The Steppe never taught us to fight the sea itself," he thought grimly. "But storms are storms, and storms can be weathered."

Darek's daggers gleamed faintly, his knuckles white. His first instinct was to laugh, curse, or spit in defiance — but no sound left him. Only the cold realization that this was a fight where his cunning might not be enough. *Still, better to drown fighting than waiting.*

Kaelorin closed his eyes, his hum soft but steady. He had seen echoes of the king in the drowned knights — sorrow, regret, love for his people. That love had been shackled into corruption. "He is not only monster," he murmured to himself. "But if he rises fully, he will end us."

Silent Resolve

They exchanged glances through the rope that bound them.
Kaelen lifted his flame, forcing it steady. **Together.**
Lysera pressed her hand to her heart, then to Kaelen's arm. **Trust.**

Darek tapped both daggers, then pointed them at the king. **Fight.**

Ravyn angled his spear forward. **Strike first.**

Kaelorin's hum deepened, resonating through each of them. **Endure.**

The drowned king raised his scepter. The hall shook, pillars cracking, currents howling. Chains of light still clung to his limbs, but now they writhed like living serpents, striking outward with deadly reach.

Kaelen's chest burned as Serenya's whisper surged into him, fierce and unyielding:

"Yes. Face him. For what you fight here is not just the shard, not just the king, but despair itself. Break it — or be drowned by it."

The companions braced, weapons raised, hearts steadied.

The battle was about to begin.

Chapter Seventy-Five

The Drowned King's Wrath

Vengeance Wakes Beneath the Waves

The throne hall shook as the drowned king rose fully, chains writhing like serpents around his limbs. His eyes blazed violet, shards of the Eclipsera pulsing inside his chest. The sea itself bent at his command, currents thrashing the companions as though they were insects.

This was no simple foe. This was a battle that would break in stages — each one dragging them deeper into the heart of corruption.

Stage One — The Chains Awaken

The king's broken scepter struck the floor, and the glowing chains lashed outward. They moved with terrifying speed, striking not like bindings but like living whips. One caught Ravyn across the chest, hurling him back into a pillar. Another coiled around Lysera's staff, trying to wrench it from her grip.

Kaelen's flame seared through one, the rope linking them the only thing keeping her from being dragged away. Darek slashed furiously, cutting through links of light that splintered into shards and dissolved. Kaelorin's hum steadied them, vibrating through the rope, reminding them: **hold together.**

Each chain they broke dimmed the light in the king's eyes, but he roared soundlessly, the entire hall trembling in fury.

Stage Two — The Current's Fury

As the chains fell, the king raised his scepter. The water itself turned against them. A violent current surged, pulling them toward the shattered floor. Bubbles tore from their mouths, lungs burning.

Kaelen drove his flame into the current, boiling a path forward. Lysera summoned roots and kelp to anchor them to broken pillars. Darek wrapped the rope around his arm, snarling as it cut into his flesh, refusing to let go.

Ravyn planted his spear in the stone, bracing against the tide. "Ride the storm!" his eyes screamed, even beneath the waves.

Kaelorin raised his staff, a soft starlight rippling outward, calming the worst of the currents, giving them breath enough to endure. Still, the pressure crushed against them, threatening to break bones and will alike.

Stage Three — The King Revealed

The current ebbed, and for the first time the king moved forward. His towering form loomed above them, his crown of coral gleaming, his face twisted into a mask of sorrow and rage.

He opened his mouth — and a torrent of drowned voices spilled out, filling the water with their wails. The sound was not heard but *felt*, pressing into their chests, whispering:

"Join us... drown with us... let go..."

Kaelen faltered, his flame flickering. Lysera's vines blackened, nearly snapping. Darek's grip loosened.

Only Kaelorin's voice answered, his hum rising into a song of stars. It wove through the water, striking against the drowned chorus. For a heartbeat, Kaelen saw the king's true face — weary, regal, sorrowful — before the shard's corruption blazed brighter, twisting him back into a monster.

Preparing for the Final Stage

The companions regrouped, battered but unbroken. Their rope strained, their bodies ached, but their eyes met in fierce resolve.

Kaelen clenched the shard in his palm, flame blazing steady once more.

Lysera lifted her staff, her vines trembling but alive.

Darek readied his daggers, blood swirling from his cut arm.

Ravyn spun his spear, eyes alight with fury.

Kaelorin's starlight burned bright, his voice unyielding.

The drowned king raised his scepter high, chains snapping free around him. The shard's pulse thundered in their chests, demanding surrender.

Serenya's whisper cut through the storm, sharp and fierce:

"This is it. His sorrow, his fury, his corruption — all bound to the shard. Break him, and the shard is yours. Fail... and the sea will never release you."

The final stage loomed.

Chapter Seventy-Six

Fury in the Deep

Where Silence Erupts in Wrath

The drowned king raised his shattered scepter. The shard embedded in his chest flared blinding violet, its pulse reverberating through the hall and into the companions' bones. The sea howled with him — not merely water, but corruption itself, alive and furious.

The Opening Wave

With a sweep of his scepter, a tidal surge erupted inside the hall. Pillars snapped like reeds, and the companions were hurled backward. The rope strained but held, dragging them together as the current threatened to smash them against stone.

Kaelen thrust his flame forward, boiling a shield through the water, forcing a pocket of light around them. "Hold the line!"

Ravyn drove his spear into the silted floor, anchoring them against the tide. Lysera's vines erupted, binding broken masonry into a barrier. Darek clung to the rope, knives flashing to cut debris as it spiraled toward them. Kaelorin's starlight pulsed, steadying their hearts against despair.

The wave broke — but the king strode closer, chains snapping, his eyes burning brighter.

Shard-Born Power

The drowned king pointed his scepter, and shards of violet light shot like spears through the water. One tore through Lysera's barrier, grazing her side. Another shattered against Darek's blade, nearly wrenching it from his hand.

Kaelen roared bubbles, his flame intercepting a blast, the clash of fire and shard-light boiling the sea into steam. He winced as the shard in his own hand screamed in resonance, threatening to rip free.

"He's drawing from it!" Kaelen thought, panic threatening to choke him. "Every strike is the shard itself fighting us."

The Companions' Counter

Ravyn surged forward, spear spinning. He slammed it into the king's chain-wrapped arm, sparks of rune-light erupting. "Even kings bleed!" his eyes burned, though the sea swallowed his words.

Lysera's staff glowed green, kelp binding the king's legs, holding him still for a heartbeat. Darek darted upward, daggers slashing at the chain-crown, chipping coral from the king's skull.

Kaelorin's song swelled, filling the water with harmony, striking against the shard's corrupted pulse. For an instant, the drowned king faltered, his violet eyes flickering with sorrow.

"Now!" Kaelorin urged.

The Breaking Point

Kaelen hurled his flame with everything he had left. Blue fire seared through the water, straight into the shard embedded in the king's chest. The entire hall blazed with violet and azure light as corruption and fire clashed, the impact shaking stone and silt alike.

The drowned king staggered, chains flailing, the shard cracking faintly under the assault.

Serenya's whisper tore through the storm:

"Strike together! Now — or the sea will never release him!"

Bound by rope, bound by choice, the companions gathered for one final strike.

Chapter
Seventy-Seven

The Weight of
Silence

The Echo of All That Was Lost

T he shard in the drowned king's chest cracked faintly under
their united strike, its violet glow faltering. For a heartbeat, the
massive figure staggered — and in that instant, Kaelen dared to hope.
But the king was not finished.

The Shard's Last Fury

With a soundless roar, the drowned king drove his scepter into the seafloor. The shard flared violently, cracks racing across its surface. The water surged into chaos.

Currents slammed them apart, the rope binding them straining nearly to breaking. Pillars snapped and crashed, rubble scattering like meteors. From the cracks in the throne hall's floor, new chains of light erupted, lashing out with vicious speed.

One coiled around Lysera's waist, yanking her down toward the abyss. Another struck Ravyn's leg, pulling him into the silt. Darek's dagger-arm was seized, his blade shattered as he struggled furiously.

Kaelen's flame guttered, nearly smothered by the whirlpool of power. The shard in his palm screamed in resonance, threatening to fuse with the king's.

Visions of Drowning

As the king's eyes blazed brighter, the shard poured visions into their minds.

- **Kaelen** saw himself sinking, his flame fading until only darkness remained.

- **Lysera** saw her vines rotting, strangling her friends one by one.

- **Darek** saw himself slashing the rope, leaving the others to drown while he fled.

- **Ravyn** saw the Steppe burning again, his people's ashes scattering across the waves.

- **Kaelorin** saw the stars blink out, the sky collapsing into endless night.

Their hearts faltered. Their breath burned. For a moment, despair itself felt heavier than the sea.

Holding the Line

But even in the storm, Kaelorin's hum trembled out, faint but resolute. It rippled through the rope, through their hands, reminding them: *You are not alone.*

Kaelen clenched his fist, forcing his flame to blaze, burning through the chain that dragged Lysera down. Ravyn braced his spear against the silt, breaking his chain with a surge of fury. Darek tore free with a savage twist, blood streaming from his arm, eyes burning with defiance. Lysera's staff shone, green light surging into Kaelen's flame, steadying it.

Together, they resisted the shard's last desperate grasp.

The Moment Before the End

The drowned king staggered again, but his form did not crumble. His crown of coral gleamed, his scepter raised high, his chains writhing like serpents. The shard in his chest pulsed wild and unstable, its light tearing the water apart.

Kaelen raised his flame. The others gathered beside him, weapons steady, rope binding them tight.

Serenya's whisper surged through the dream-currents, fierce as thunder:

"Now! One final strike — together — or the sea will claim you!"

The battle's end was upon them.

Chapter
Seventy-Eight

The Shard
Claimed

The Flame Taken, the Balance Trembles

The drowned king loomed above them, his crown of coral blazing, his chest split by the violet shard's pulse. Chains writhed like serpents, the water itself tearing in his fury. Yet the companions held — bound by rope, by trust, by choice.

Kaelen's flame burned steady in his palm. Lysera's staff glowed with green light. Darek's daggers flashed sharp despite blood loss. Ravyn's spear spun like a storm. Kaelorin's staff sang starlight into the deep.

For a moment, all five hearts beat as one.

The Final Strike

Kaelen surged forward, flame searing brighter than ever, not fading but blazing in defiance of the sea.

Lysera wrapped his fire in roots and kelp, binding it into a spear of living flame.

Darek slashed through the last chains, clearing the path with a cry of fury.

Ravyn drove his spear alongside Kaelen's fire, piercing the drowned king's chest.

Kaelorin's starlight poured into the strike, harmony meeting sorrow.

Together, their powers converged — fire, life, steel, storm, and star — striking straight into the shard.

The drowned king's eyes widened. For one breath, his sorrow showed through the corruption, as if he remembered who he had once been.

Then the shard cracked.

The Breaking of the King

Light erupted, violet shattering into azure, flooding the hall with blinding radiance. The drowned king roared without sound, his body splitting apart into brine and shadow. His scepter crumbled, his crown dissolved into coral dust, his chains unraveled into nothing.

The colossal figure collapsed into the silt, then dissolved into silence.

The shard hovered in the water, freed at last — jagged, glowing faintly blue where once it burned violet, its pulse calmer, steadier.

Kaelen reached for it, and as his flame touched the crystal, it fused with the shard he already bore. A surge of warmth coursed through him — not only power, but memory.

Visions flashed: the drowned city as it once was, proud and radiant; the king standing tall, a protector who chose to sacrifice himself to bind the shard. His last thought echoed: *Forgive me.*

Kaelen gasped, holding the shard close.

Aftermath in the Deep

The hall grew quiet. The currents stilled. The storm's pull faded.

The companions floated together, exhausted but unbroken, the rope between them slack but unsevered. Lysera's hand brushed Kaelen's arm, steadying him. Darek's blood drifted in the water, but his smirk was tired and real. Ravyn braced on his spear, unbowed. Kaelorin's hum softened, carrying peace instead of warning.

Serenya's whisper filled them all, warm and proud:

"Yes. You have done what few could — faced sorrow, broken corruption, and claimed hope from it. The shard is yours. But know this: each one you reclaim carries not only power, but the burden of what was lost. Bear it well."

The shard pulsed in Kaelen's palm, brighter now. One step closer to wholeness. One step closer to dawn.

And the drowned halls of Veyra's Fall fell silent once more.

Chapter Seventy-Nine

The Generals Stir

The Slumber of Tyrants Breaks

T he Obsidian Spire pulsed with the fractured glow of the Eclipsera. The shards mounted upon its black altar suddenly flickered — one light dimming, another shifting from violet to azure. The entire chamber trembled.

The Draconis generals felt it at once.

The Black Dragon

From the shadows along the wall, the Black Dragon's ember-eyes flared. His voice was a hiss of stone grinding.

"They took it. The drowned shard is theirs."

He turned slowly, rage simmering in silence. "And the guardian bound to it is gone. The sea's fury, broken."

The Azure Dragon

The Azure Dragon tilted his mirrored helm, voice rippling like water. "Impossible. The drowned king was chained by his own people, fused with sorrow itself. No mortal fire or vine could unmake him."

Yet even his illusions could not deny the truth — the shard's pulse was weaker.

The Red Dragon

The Red Dragon's armored fists clenched, heat hissing from his scales. "Twice now they scar us. First me, now the sea's champion. These whelps steal from us what was forged in blood. I say we burn the Steppe itself until they crawl out begging for mercy!"

The Silver Dragon

Laughter echoed from the Silver Dragon, sharp as a blade drawn in silence. "No. Let them rise higher. Let them gather hope, gather shards, gather allies. The higher they climb, the harder they break when we tear it away."

His smile gleamed beneath his helm. "But perhaps... it is time we ceased waiting."

Avarith's Command

The Dark Lord rose from his throne, his black armor glowing faint with the veins of the Stone. His voice silenced them all.

"Enough. They endure because each of you toys with them — tests them, waits for them to stumble. But their victories are not weakness; they are cracks in our dominion."

He turned his helm toward the Black Dragon. "They have defied your shadow."

Toward the Azure. "They have resisted your illusions."

Toward the Red. "They have scarred your fire."

His gauntlet slammed onto the altar, making the shards scream.

"The next time you strike them — do not test. Do not toy. Break them."

The generals bowed, silence hanging heavy in the Spire.

Serenya's Sensing

In her crystal, Serenya felt the ripple of Avarith's fury. Her fur bristled, her glow trembling. For the first time, she dared to hope her whispers had reached far enough.

"Yes... the cracks spread even among them. Hold fast, Kaelen. Hold fast, all of you. Their fury only proves they fear you now."

The tide of battle was shifting.

Chapter Eighty

The Shard Rises

The Flame Ascends, Shadows Follow

T he water parted with a violent rush, and one by one the companions burst into the open air.

The storm still raged above, lightning splitting violet across the clouds, waves crashing against the broken spires. Yet compared to the silence of the drowned halls, the air felt like a rebirth.

Gasping for Air

Kaelen heaved, dragging in breath after breath, his chest burning from the depths below. The shard pulsed faintly in his hand, its violet glow now tempered by a softer azure, as though purified by their struggle.

Lysera clung to the raft they had left tethered to the spire, her staff still glowing weakly, eyes brimming with both exhaustion and relief. "We made it," she gasped. "By the Light... we truly made it."

Darek flopped against the boards, coughing seawater, blood swirling from his cut arm. He still managed a crooked grin. "Never... want to swim again. Next time, I'm robbing a ship."

Ravyn hauled himself up, bracing his spear against the raft. His eyes burned as he scanned the storm-lashed horizon. "The sea tried to claim us. It failed."

Kaelorin surfaced last, calm as ever, though his face was pale from strain. He laid a hand on the shard in Kaelen's grip, murmuring softly, "It remembers what it was. And it mourns what it became."

The Sea's Reaction

As they steadied themselves, the storm shifted. The winds lessened, the lightning dimmed, and the waves grew calmer — as if the ocean itself recognized that something long corrupted had been freed.

The drowned city still jutted from the waves, but its spires no longer burned with violet glow. They were only ruins now, broken teeth in a quiet sea.

Lysera whispered, almost reverently, "We ended it. The king's sorrow is finally at rest."

Kaelen held the shard higher, its light gleaming against the fading storm. "Another piece reclaimed."

Serenya's Whisper

From her crystal prison, Serenya's voice reached them clearly, proud and steady:

"Yes. You rise not just with a shard, but with hope renewed. Remember — each victory breaks their hold a little more. And each shard you claim brings us closer to dawn."

Kaelen closed his fist around the shard, meeting the eyes of his companions. For all their wounds, their doubts, their scars — they endured.

Together, they turned their raft toward the horizon.

The sea was behind them. The next trial waited ahead.

Chapter Eighty-One

The First Ripple

The Beginning of the Endless Wave

The sea calmed behind them, its storm subdued. The shard pulsed faintly in Kaelen's hand, no longer violet with corruption but burning soft blue, a steady light in the dark. For the first time since their journey began, the companions felt as though they had truly torn something free from the Draconis grasp.

But the world itself felt it too.

Across the Realms

In distant villages that had known only silence and ash, the wind shifted, carrying whispers of hope. Fires long thought unquenchable guttered. Water once brackish ran clear. For a fleeting moment, the universes bound to the Stone shuddered — not in collapse, but in renewal.

Elders looked to the skies, feeling echoes of a balance thought lost. Children stirred from dreams of despair to see faint light piercing through the endless night.

The ripple spread, unseen but undeniable.

In the Obsidian Spire

The altar screamed. Shards of the Eclipsera flared unevenly, their once perfect harmony fractured by the liberation of another piece. The chamber shook, and the generals gathered in unease.

The **Red Dragon** snarled, his armor blazing. "Twice now they wound us. Shall we watch as they shatter us piece by piece?"

The **Azure Dragon**'s mirrored helm glimmered faint. "This ripple... it strengthens them, and weakens us. Even illusions cannot veil it."

The **Black Dragon**'s ember-eyes burned with fury. "Shadows do not break. Yet they endured me. And now the sea itself bends to them."

The **Silver Dragon** only smiled, though even his cruel amusement was strained. "Cracks spread. And once cracks form, walls fall. Tell me, brothers — is it the fox's whispers we fear, or the storm gathering against us?"

Their voices fell silent as the **Dark Lord Avarith** rose, his gauntleted hand closing around the shards. The light bled through his grip, violent and unstable.

His voice thundered like iron.

"They are emboldened. The worlds stir. But know this: hope is as fragile as glass. One strike, and it shatters. We will break them before the dawn can rise."

Serenya in the Crystal

In her prison of crystal, Serenya felt it — the ripple through the dream-currents, the faint warmth of the shard's light restored. Her fur bristled, her eyes shone bright.

She whispered into the void, not only to Kaelen but to every world still trembling:

"Yes... let them stir. Let them hope. For hope is the blade that cuts chains. And with each shard reclaimed, the day draws nearer when I will rise again."

Closing Note

The companions rowed inland, the shard glowing in Kaelen's hand. They were exhausted, scarred, but united.

Behind them, the sea was quiet. Ahead of them, storms yet waited.

But for the first time, the world itself seemed to breathe again.

And so ended the first book of their journey — not with victory absolute, but with the **first ripple of change**, and the promise that the Draconis Order was no longer unchallenged.

Acknowledgements

This book could not have come to life without the support and encouragement of those who believed in the story from the very beginning. To the readers who journeyed with Kaelen, Lysera, Darek, Ravyn, Kaelorin, and Serenya — thank you for stepping into the universes of the Crystal Fox. Every page was written with you in mind.

Special thanks to the dreamers, storytellers, and kindred spirits who inspired this saga through countless conversations and ideas. Your passion for fantasy is the spark that keeps the flame alive.

And finally, to those who fight every day to bring a little more balance, light, and hope into the world — this story is for you.

About the author

Christopher Plummer is a storyteller, creator, and dream-builder. With a lifelong passion for epic fantasy, vaporwave aesthetics, and the blending of music, myth, and art, he founded **Crystal Fox Press** as a home for tales that bridge worlds and stir the imagination.

When not writing, Christopher explores new creative ventures across multiple mediums, from designing merchandise and art under his D3a1hXSaga brand, to producing lo-fi/vaporwave-inspired music that echoes the same sense of nostalgia and wonder found in his books.

The *Crystal Fox Saga* is his flagship fantasy epic, but it is only the beginning. His vision is a growing multiverse of interconnected stories — where balance, courage, and creativity stand against shadow.

Also by the Author

The Crystal Fox Saga: Book One is the first step in a long journey.

Coming soon:

- **The Crystal Fox Saga: Book Two** (Storms of the Fractured Realms)

- Additional works exploring the lore of the Draconis Order, the fox's whispers, and the broken worlds left in their wake.

Sneak Peek: Book Two

Chapter One: Shadows on the Steppe

"The ripple of hope has not gone unnoticed. In distant lands, the storms gather, and the Draconis generals sharpen their blades. But as cracks spread through the Order, old alliances stir — and new heroes rise to answer the fox's call..."

The Steppe winds carried a different sound now. Not only the thunder of hooves or the howl of storms — but whispers. Whispers of the drowned city, of a shard reclaimed, of the Draconis Order scarred for the first time in centuries.

The world itself had felt the ripple. And so had the generals.

Uneasy Bonds

Kaelen rode at the front, the reclaimed shard pulsing against his palm. Its glow was calmer than before, yet each beat pressed into his chest like a weight, carrying not only power but memory. The drowned king's sorrow lingered, and in his dreams Kaelen still felt the pull of water closing over him.

Behind him, the others rode in silence. Lysera's staff glowed faintly, but her eyes were distant, haunted by visions she could not shake. Darek twirled a dagger at his side, every so often glancing at the rope still tied around his arm — a reminder of bonds that had nearly broken beneath the sea. Ravyn alone looked steady, his gaze on the horizon, but even he felt the strain of carrying others into storms they could not yet weather.

Kaelorin hummed softly, as if to mend the silence. But even his star-song could not erase the shadows that now lurked between them.

The Black Dragon Hunts Again

Far behind, unseen, the Black Dragon stirred. He had failed once, and the memory of it burned. But shadows were patient, and now he wove his hunt deeper. Not with illusions of beasts or chains of fear — but with whispers of betrayal, planted in every dream.

"They will leave you."
"They will fail you."
"They will turn against you."

The companions did not speak of it. But each night, as they closed their eyes, the whispers grew louder.

Ravyn's Training

By day, Ravyn drilled them without mercy. They rode across the Steppe until their legs ached, learning the old ways of the Riders — the spear formations, the shifting flanks, the thunderous charge. He drove them to fight as one, to strike and move like the storm.

But even as their blades found rhythm, their hearts faltered. For every moment of unity, a shadow lingered at the edge of trust. Kaelen caught Darek's stare too long. Lysera's vines recoiled when Kaelen's flame brushed them. Ravyn noticed it all, but said nothing — for to name it might make it real.

The Silver Dragon Stirs

Far away, the Silver Dragon smiled. He had waited long for his moment, letting the others burn, rot, and rage. Now the cracks had formed — and where cracks formed, he would slide his blade.

He whispered into the currents, sowing doubt across fractured realms, turning allies into rivals before they ever reached the field. His voice was not flame or shadow, but honey laced with venom.

"Trust no one fully. Trust me instead."

A Glimpse of What's Coming

That night, Kaelen dreamed again of Serenya. Her form shimmered in crystal, her tails wrapped around her like a shield. Her eyes burned fierce as ever, yet even her light wavered.

"Kaelen," she whispered, her voice strained. *"Every shard you reclaim weakens me as much as it frees me. The cracks spread through them... and through me. Beware the Silver one — for he strikes not with strength, but with trust itself."*

The dream shattered, leaving Kaelen gasping. The shard in his hand pulsed hot, searing him, as if to remind him: power always demands a cost.

And in the distance, storm clouds gathered over the fractured realms.

A Call to Readers

Thank you for reading *The Crystal Fox Saga: Book One*!

If you enjoyed this story, please consider leaving a review on Amazon, Goodreads, or your favorite platform. Reviews are the lifeblood of independent authors and help new readers discover the saga.

Your voice helps keep the flame alive.